IN TIME FOR CHRISTMAS

A TIME TRAVEL WESTERN ROMANCE

HEATHER BLANTON

In Time for Christmas – A Novella

Please subscribe to my newsletter
to receive updates on my new releases and other fun news. You'll
also receive a FREE e-book—
A Lady in Defiance, The Lost Chapters
just for subscribing!

In Time for Christmas – A Novella

Published by Rivulet Publishing

Kindle Edition

Copyright 2013 Heather Blanton

Cover Photography Courtesy Library of Congress
Scripture taken from the HOLY BIBLE,

KING JAMES VERSION - PUBLIC DOMAIN

Thank you DiAne Gates, Terri Sullivan, Mary Holland, Meredith Drake,
Jeannette Shields, Margit Moran, Heather Baker, Tammy Wall, Grace
Thompson, Debbie Haigler, Tonja Saylor, Jennifer Kimble, Brenda McMillion
– the best beta readers a gal could have. Thank you!

Heather Blanton

Please subscribe to my newsletter
https://www.subscribepage.com/z8i1i3_copy
to receive updates on my new releases and other fun news.
You'll also receive a FREE e-book—
A Lady in Defiance, The Lost Chapters
just for subscribing!

9 And Isaiah said, This sign shalt thou have of the LORD, that the LORD will do the thing that he hath spoken: shall the shadow go forward ten degrees, or go back ten degrees?

10 And Hezekiah answered, It is a light thing for the shadow to go down ten degrees: nay, but let the shadow return backward ten degrees. *2 Kings Chapter 20*

CHAPTER 1

$\mathcal{T}$he vicious slap sent Charlene spinning to the floor. She squeezed her eyes shut and tried to focus on the heated Spanish tile pressing against her cheek, not the fireworks exploding in her head. The familiar black fog threatened to claim her, but she fought it. He did such terrible things to her when she lost consciousness ...

"I told you, Charlene," Dale loomed over her, wagging an accusing finger, "If you talked to him anymore, I'd break something. Is that what you want? You want me to break something?"

Charlene squinted up at him. A vein throbbed in his temple, the subtle sign he was on the verge of losing control. Straight, dark hair fell haphazardly over his icy blue eyes. He would have looked boyish and charming if not for the sneer curling his lip.

She swallowed and slowly pushed her way to her hands and knees. "He's the mail man, Dale. We were just talking." Her explanation was pointless. She knew it, yet she could never stop defending herself. Perhaps it was one small way of keeping her spirit alive. A little dash of rebellion. "He comes by here the same time every day."

Dale wrapped his fingers in her disheveled mess of blonde hair and jerked her the rest of the way to her feet. She winced, grabbed at his hand, but didn't make a sound. Charlene didn't hate Dale. But she wasn't afraid of him, either.

She simply felt nothing.

She'd learned a long time ago that Dale was greedy for control. Fear, or any emotion at all, gave it to him. After a particularly vicious beating six months ago, she had vowed he would never see a spark of anything in her ever again.

He stared at her hard, like a bear debating whether to attack or walk away, and after a moment, tossed her aside. He turned his back on her and dragged his hands through his hair. Charlene took a deep breath and pulled herself up to her full, impressive height of 5'3". Yes, Dale fancied himself a real man. Broad-shouldered and handsome, he liked expensive suits because they flattered his body-builder physique and lean rear end. And in his world, men beat up women half their size.

"I'm not putting up with it anymore, Charlene."

"Then let me go, Dale." *Oh, God, please, I just want out.* "At least let me go home for Christmas." She regretted the words the moment they slipped out of her mouth. Anything she really wanted converted to leverage for Dale.

He turned to her, grinning with amusement. Brushing a speck of dust off his tailored sleeve, he laughed at her slip. Another victory for him. "Home. Yeah, you know, that's an excellent idea. I'll take you home."

Three days later, Dale burst in from work, tossed his brief case to the leather Ikea couch, and dropped his hands on his hips. Charlene, stirring spaghetti sauce on the stove with all the passion of a robot, dragged her gaze over to him. Triumph glowed on his face.

Something very bad was about to happen. But, strangely, she found the fear exhilarating. She'd purged the tears, the prayers, and the hope in one long, dark night months ago. Now, even though she felt like she was dying on the inside, he would never see past her stony face again. She set down the spoon and faced him.

"Pack," he said. "I'm taking you home."

———

The light from the BMW's dashboard lit Dale's face with a ghostly, green glow as he stared ahead at the dark highway. He reminded her of a man possessed. Was he going to kill her? He peered over at her and smiled a cold, soulless grin that convinced her she'd better start thinking about escape.

She was locked in the car with Satan and Satan drove all night. He did stop once for gas and cheerfully asked her if she wanted anything. His smile was chilling. Charlene shook her head, squashing her appetite along with her emotions.

At some point, she actually dozed off. When she awoke, dull evergreens, fiery orange maple trees and blazing yellow oaks filled her vision. All around, the leaves flamed with color. She looked up through the sunroof and saw a mountain towering over them. Hope rising, she swung her gaze back out the passenger side window and waited for a break in the trees along the interstate. Soon, she caught glimpses of a deep, wide valley splashed with brilliant fall color. She didn't see any ski slopes carved on the steep mountainsides. In fact, she didn't she see much in the way of civilization at all. She frowned. Were they near Ouray, maybe?

She'd barely spoken all night, but ventured a question now. "Where are we going?"

He took an exit ramp and the road morphed easily from

sweeping interstate to a wide, winding dragon's tail that rose upward. Dale dropped the BMW into a lower gear and chuckled. "I told you, I'm taking you home."

A sinking feeling pulled Charlene deeper into the black leather. Twisting words is what Dale did for a living. What all lawyers did for a living. "OK," she nodded, "Whose home? What home?"

Again, the chuckle that trumpeted his sense of victory. "My family's ranch."

Charlene turned her head to the window to hide her shock. The Page family ranch, four hundred acres of isolated mountain land so steep barely half of it had ever been cultivated. Four generations of the family had eked out a living on it till Dale's father Roy, sick of the pointless, hard-scrabble existence, had abandoned the ranch in 1968. He had leased it sporadically up until about ten years ago. Cursing his grandfather for being a poor businessman, Roy had turned his back on the rural life and raised his children on the paved streets of Denver.

Dale had been trying to figure out what to do with the property since he'd inherited it some six months ago. He said the land was so steep and rocky it didn't make much sense to subdivide it. The homes would cost too much to build. And there really wasn't enough pasture for a profitable-sized herd of cattle. The ranch *was* extremely remote, though. For the right buyer, Dale believed that could be a plus. He had plenty of wealthy clients who preferred their privacy.

In the throes of deciding the ranch's fate, he had stripped the house bare, selling every table, appliance, rug, light fixture, door knob, and bed frame for whatever cash he could get. The house itself was so rundown, he'd almost bull-dozed it. The memories of a few fun summers at the place had strummed his heartstrings, or so he'd claimed, and he'd given the structure a reprieve. Temporarily.

So why was he taking her there? To bury her beneath the rocks and pines of some lonely canyon?

He drove for another hour, the road rising more noticeably now, winding and twisting up, up into the mountains. Well-maintained paved roads gave way to narrow, crumbling paved roads, then to gravel, and, with the last turn, to a narrow, rutted dirt road.

When his bumper scraped, Dale pulled over. "We'll walk from here."

Charlene slowly unfolded herself from the little sports car and pulled her suitcase from what BMW laughingly referred to as the back seat. She surveyed the tall, dense ponderosa pines and oversized hardwoods surrounding her, rising above her like guards on the steep mountainsides. They should have made her feel lonely. Instead, she found some comfort in the way they watched over things.

She zipped her fleece hoodie against the chill and started walking. As they clambered up the dirt road full of switchbacks, ruts and large, misplaced rocks, Dale cursed behind her. Charlene smiled to herself. He was still wearing business attire. His Paciotti loafers slipped and scraped for traction on the loose rock and dirt, working a steady string of curses out of him. She had on her blue Merrells and her traction was more than sufficient.

As they hiked, she noticed the huffing and puffing from him growing more pronounced. The steep road and ridiculously inappropriate shoes were really taking it out of him. It occurred to her it would be easy to swing her suitcase around, knock him clean unconscious with it, and skip back down to the car. Leave him here in the boonies. See how he liked it.

As the thought tried to take root, Dale spoke, sucking wind like an old man. "When you get to the top of this ridge

... you can see the whole thing ... The house ... the fields ... all of it."

She thought about her plan a second more but stored it away and picked up her pace. A minute later she reached the ridge. Here, the trees fell away and a small valley unrolled before her. The land was flat as a pancake and sandwiched between two ridges of blazing, jagged mountains that practically erupted up out of the ground. Below her, the two-story farmhouse sat sagging, forlorn and abandoned, beside a wide, healthy creek that cut through the valley. Three dilapidated log out-buildings dotted the pasture, and one large, collapsing barn, a cedar structure of milled timber, loomed over the barn yard. Acres and acres of fields that once grew crops now only held the bones of dried corn stalks, weeds and saplings.

Charlene clutched a maple branch as she took a step forward and surveyed the magnificent vista. If not for the shaggy grass, weedy pastures, and saggy buildings, it could have been a photograph right out of Our State magazine. In spite of the flaws, she saw the homestead's beauty and felt ... peace.

As if timed to impress her, the sun broke through the billowy gray clouds above and Charlene gasped. In the suddenly brilliant light, the place *transformed*. Freshly-painted, tidy, and as full of promise as the first Page ancestor had believed. She watched awestruck as a woman, dressed in a long skirt, tossed scratch to the chickens milling around the barn. In the corral, a man trotted a palomino around in a circle as another man hung on the fence observing.

Confounded by the visions, Charlene blinked and shook her head

And the ranch returned to its' broken, hopeless present.

Heart racing, she placed a hand over her mouth. What

had she just seen? A trick of the light? A stress-induced mirage? Was she simply losing her mind?

But it had looked so real.

"Move it." She started as Dale, still gasping for breath, smacked her on the bottom. "I don't have all day."

Charlene wandered slowly through the old home, wondering about the generations of family that had lived here. She closed her eyes and tried to listen for their laughter, or catch a whiff of pipe smoke. The rooms were completely empty but the faded remnants of tattered wallpaper still decorated the front parlor and the wall along the stairs. Lighter rectangle and oval shapes told her pictures had once hung here and there.

Apparently never covered, the kitchen walls were bare, revealing the basic log structure of the home. Nothing remained in this room except part of the stove pipe dangling from the ceiling and some cobwebs. A missing back door and a large, broken window opened up on the overgrown back yard, allowing a view to the barn and another smaller building. The outhouse?

She meandered back to the front room, the parlor, and ran her hands over the smooth river rock fireplace. Her thoughts drifted. Absently rubbing her shoulders against the fall chill, she imagined a piano sitting cozily in the corner between the fireplace and side window. Scratches and dust covered the pine floor, but she could see the wear from long forgotten footsteps at the front entrance and the doorway to the kitchen. A large bay window looked out across the front porch to the yard and beyond. The glass was mostly gone and the floor was soft and rotting. A massive oak blocked

7

most of the view of the distant mountains. She could imagine sitting beneath its large, shady branches, sipping tea and watching a child play on a rope swing.

Strangely calm, she turned back to the parlor. A simple, quaint room, she liked it, though she couldn't say why. Nothing was left to tell her if the original Victorian furnishings had ever given way to the chrome and vinyl of the fifties or shag carpet of the sixties. Somehow she doubted it. No one had ever installed electricity in the home, other than a generator that powered a range and refrigerator. She thought it a safe bet no one would have bothered with redecorating the house.

As she pondered the other Pages and their lives here, Dale stormed through the front door. He marched from room to room, opening and slamming doors, checking closets, then hurried upstairs. He stomped around up there, repeating his search. The floor creaked loudly under his weight. Charlene heard him grunt occasionally, perhaps satisfied the house was truly empty.

He descended the stairs in a rush and disappeared outside again. She listened to his loafers pitter-patter across the porch and then fade away. A few moments later, he came back and stood in the door way. "All right, I'm leaving."

"What?" She spun away from the fireplace to face him. "What do you mean you're leaving? You're leaving me here? Alone?"

Dale shoved his right hand into his pocket and grinned like a movie star. "Baby, you said you wanted to go home for Christmas."

"It's October!" Anger that she hadn't let herself feel in a long time boiled up and the steam found its way to her voice. "You think I'm just going to stay here? Waiting for you? There's no food. There's no heat. You can't leave me here. I'll starve."

Dale's blue eyes stormed and his lips thinned into an angry line. He crossed the room and grabbed Charlene's jaw, shoving her back against the rocks. "I bet when I come back, you won't have a thought left in your pretty little head about *Harvey* the mail man." He pinched her cheeks tighter and she ground her teeth to keep from crying out. "I bet you'll be glad to see me."

She jerked free and glared at him. "I've talked to the man twice. About YOUR Amazon deliveries. What is the matter with you?"

Dale never liked to have his sanity questioned, his reason doubted. After all this time, she knew that, but some fighters didn't know when to say uncle. He moved closer to her, their noses almost touching, his face contorting into an ugly mask. "There are four hundred acres of wilderness, mountain lions, and maybe even grizzlies between you and the closest neighbor. Now, I'll be back in a few days to check on you. If you greet me in an appropriate manner, maybe you can change your future and come home. But till then—"

Dale drew back and punched Charlene. She never saw his hand, just felt the starburst of pain which was smothered almost instantly by darkness.

CHAPTER 2

"*D*ear, dear, *dear* me," a woman fretted.

Charlene's first thought was that she had fallen asleep with the TV on. Some old movie? Glass clinked and then something warm and damp touched her forehead. It felt so comforting she hated to wake up ... only to look into Dale's face. If he was touching her with anything other than violence, that meant he only wanted one thing.

"Your color is returning at least." Charlene's eyes flew open. "Oh, lovely, you're coming 'round." A woman, roughly in her late sixties, early seventies, slightly pudgy, a loose bun of gray hair piled atop her head, sat on the edge of the couch and aimed a warm smile at Charlene. "Perhaps we won't need the doctor after all. I was just about to send Billy."

Charlene swallowed and looked around a cozy parlor, shadows from the fire dancing erratically on the walls. She glanced out the bay window but couldn't see anything but darkness.

The woman chuckled. "Honey, your eyes are as big as saucers. There's nothing to be concerned about. You're all right now."

Now?

Where was she? What was going on here? Was Dale pulling some kind of trick on her? He did the most awful things to her when she was unconscious. She preferred cigarette burns, though, to this confusion. Eager to stop whatever was happening, she clawed her way to a sitting position. The woman pulled the cloth from her head and situated the pillows behind Charlene's back.

Charlene's glance ricocheted crazily around the room. It *looked* like the parlor at the Page ranch but she couldn't be sure. The wallpaper pattern of stripes and roses matched the wallpaper she'd seen earlier. Only this wallpaper was brand new, the pattern crisp and clear, and was neatly glued to the walls. The room and its nineteenth century furnishings were pristine, straight out of a museum. The fireplace of smooth, round river rock could pass as the same, too. Charlene rubbed her forehead, frightened and confused. "Where am I? What's going on here?"

The elderly woman spoke gently, cautiously. "You don't remember? My grandson found you wandering around in our cornfield." She regarded Charlene with a mix of fear and compassion. "Oh, maybe we should get the doctor. Do you think you bumped your head?"

Charlene scrubbed her face with her hands and shook her head. "I don't know anything," she said, through her fingers. "I was standing at the fireplace and Dale hit me," the woman gasped and Charlene peeked at her, "Then I woke up here. Where is here?"

"You're on the Page ranch. My grandson's ranch."

Charlene dropped her hands into her lap and held her face completely still. So this was all some elaborate, cruel joke. And this lady was in on it.

She studied the room again. Chippendale coffee table, kerosene lamp glowing softly over their heads, a roll top desk in the corner, a small piano to the left of the fireplace. She paused to consider the instrument. Somehow, seeing it made her feel better. It belonged in this room. She drifted a hand over the golden settee she was resting on and then noticed her skirt. She picked up a handful of the, what, muslin? She rubbed the sky blue material between her fingers and wagged her head in amazement.

What an incredible job. The walls were patched, the room painted and wallpapered, the furniture matched perfectly for the early 1900's. Someone had even changed her clothes. This had to have taken a while to complete. How long was she out? A panicky feeling tried charging at her heart. "So what am I supposed to do?" She lifted her chin and spoke with as much calm as she could muster. "Just play along?"

"I beg your pardon?" The woman sounded confused. "Play along with what?"

Charlene's heart sank. The lady had been paid to play a role. Couldn't blame her for not deviating from it. Not if she wanted to ever see the money.

The woman rose and stepped out of the way as Charlene swung her feet to the floor.

Wringing her hands, she asked, "Can I get you anything? Are you hungry or thirsty?"

"You're allowed to feed me?"

The woman's brow shot up, but a look of understanding and compassion quickly replaced the surprise. She sat down again and took Charlene's hands in hers. "My name is Kate Page. Everyone calls me Miss Kate." She squeezed Charlene's hands. "I don't know what you're running from, but I can guess. And I can promise you, you're safe here." Charlene was taken aback by the sincerity in Miss Kate's voice. She was a fine actress. She had to give her credit.

"Where is Dale?" Charlene asked wearily, unwilling to play this game or fall for the woman's warmth.

"Is Dale your husband?"

Charlene sighed, but before she could respond, the front door opened and a man stepped into the shadowy foyer.

"That you, Billy?" Miss Kate asked over her shoulder.

"Yes, ma'am." The man removed his coat and hat, hung them on the pegs next to the front door then strode into the parlor. Charlene was not surprised to see that this new player was Dale. She figured he hadn't gone far. The vintage tan trousers, black vest, and blue striped shirt didn't impress her, but she did wonder how he had managed to grow out his hair and change its color to a lighter, caramel hue with more waves in it. And his sleeves were rolled up. Dale hated that and always folded them instead.

A creeping fear slithered up her spine.

"Oh, she's awake," he said, sounding pleased.

Dale stepped closer to them and the light revealed more disturbing details. Charlene couldn't help but stare. This was Dale, of course, yet something was different. He looked … younger. More like twenty-six instead of thirty-six. The stubbly, square jaw, ice-blue eyes, and broad shoulders were similar, too, but not the same. The softer curve to his lips, the easier, more relaxed walk, the alert, but gentle appraisal he gave her, all that was … different.

But none of it changed who he was, what he'd done to her … or what he was trying to pull now. "Yes, I'm awake, but I'm not playing along."

Dale glanced at his grandmother then back to Charlene.

"Did you think I would just fall into this skit? Beat me all you want, but I'm not a puppet. And you can't make me think I'm crazy, Dale."

Dale worked his jaw back and forth and rested a hand on the gun at his hip. He looked at the older woman again and shrugged. "Guess I'll be fetching the doctor after all." Instead of leaving, though, he walked up to the end of the settee and

13

cocked his head a little to the left as he studied Charlene. "But, just so you know, my name isn't Dale. Don't think I like being confused with him, either. My name's Billy. Billy Page Jr., to be exact."

Charlene thought she heard the slightest hint of amusement in his voice. Dale was always laughing at her in a hard, mocking way. This sounded more like a man watching a child play. She wasn't sure she liked that much better. They stared at each other, an odd silence between them, one that puzzled Charlene. She didn't feel threatened by this man, even with the gun on his hip.

Miss Kate half-turned to her grandson. "Why don't you wait 'til morning? That's a long ride in the dark. She's not bleeding and doesn't have any broken bones." She squinted at Charlene and smiled. "Why don't we see what a good, hearty meal can accomplish?"

---

*F*eeling like the only sober person in a room full of drunks, Charlene ate the steak and fried potatoes with her head down. She sensed Billy watching her and only snatched a couple of quick glances at him. She wanted to figure this out and his similarities—or differences—with Dale rattled her. Maybe it was all just a dream, a super-vivid one. Good grief, maybe Dale had hit her so hard she was in a coma.

Miss Kate slid a plate, similarly loaded, in front of Billy and he picked up his fork. "I found you wandering in our cornfield. Strange place to find a pretty girl in a fancy dress."

Miss Kate chuckled as she sat down. "Strange place to find a girl at all, pretty or otherwise."

Charlene could tell by the way the woman's voice had faded and come back that she'd leaned into her grandson for the joke. It wasn't funny. None of this was funny. Charlene raised her head and studied the kitchen. Again, everything looked new and appropriate for the early 1900's. From the kerosene lamp in the ceiling to the ceramic-and-iron, four-burner wood stove, to the dried herbs hanging from the center beam. The three of them sat in ladder back chairs around a simple, circular kitchen table. The polished pine floor glistened and looked clean enough to eat off. No dirt or leaves or broken window. The kitchen door was intact. This felt like a *new* kitchen. So, again, she either had to be dreaming, or Dale was playing a stunningly detailed joke on her.

"Oh, I nearly forgot," Billy said, laying down his fork. "Grace." He and Kate bowed their heads and held hands as he held out a hand to Charlene … and her mouth fell open. Dale was a rabid atheist. She couldn't imagine him praying, not even for a prank. Her shock must have registered on her face. Billy looked up at her and laughed, but the sound warmed her, invited her to see the humor. "What's the matter, miss, don't they pray where you come from?"

In a moment of stark clarity, she knew without a doubt the man sitting opposite her wearing the friendly, wry smile was *not* Dale. His eyes had little lines around them, as if he'd spent more time outside in the weather. The spread of deep blue flecks in them was different, too. His hands were bigger and meatier, calloused and rough. Charlene didn't know if he was real or a dream, but he was not her husband. She closed her mouth and swallowed. "Dale doesn't pray … ever."

Another sympathetic exchange between grandson and grandmother, and then Kate reached out and lightly touched Charlene on the elbow. "I can't believe we haven't asked your name, dear."

"Charlene." She wondered crazily if she was lying on the floor of the dilapidated farmhouse, freezing to death on a fall Colorado night, but she had tasted that steak. Maybe made of fairy dust, it had tasted good and real and she wanted more. "My name is Charlene Pa—" For no reason other than a sense of caution, she decided to go with her maiden name. "Charlene Williams."

"Well, let's pray over this fine meal, Charlene," Billy said, gently taking hold of her fingers and bowing again. "And take everything else one step at a time."

She stared at his hand holding hers. Tough, calloused hands gently grasped her fingers. So different from Dale's soft, manicured hands. Charlene lowered her head and listened to Billy's deep, gentle voice lifted in prayer. It calmed her, like a loving arm around her shoulders. The words or his tone, maybe both, brought back memories of home. The friendly, smiling faces of a small town church, her father's throaty, impassioned sermons, Mama nodding her head in agreement, a quiet contentment settling over them all.

On a whim, she'd traded the peace and familiar life of a small town EMT for the drama and bustle of a Denver paramedic. It didn't take long to second-guess her choice when loneliness and homesickness started piling up on her heart like snow drifts. She met Dale at a Starbucks. Handsome, suave, successful, he won her over with a chocolate latte and a movie star smile. He showered her with lavish gifts and stunned her with such thoughtfulness that her heart didn't stand a chance. He never gave her any reason to suspect the fairy tale might end in a nightmare.

On their wedding night, Dale dropped the Prince Charming character like an actor walking off the stage. One innocent joke, a poke in his ribs, and her new husband exploded, throwing his phone at her, slapping her, screaming in her face.

Listening to Billy gently ask for a blessing on the meal, Charlene realized she hadn't prayed in over a year. God had disappeared behind a wall of fists and roaring tirades. She had let Dale block Him out. No, that wasn't fair. *She* had built the wall. Feeling stupid and ashamed that Dale had duped her so completely, so *easily*, she had curled up into a ball and shut out every emotion, especially hope.

And God was hope.

If she was lying on the floor of a dilapidated house, freezing to death from the cold, what did it matter? She couldn't find God. Couldn't find love. And she didn't care anymore. Death would simply be freedom ... wouldn't it?

---

*B*illy tried not to stare at Charlene while simultaneously ignoring his grandmother's knowing stare. For a few moments he focused on his steak. He'd fed and tended to this beef himself. He was pretty proud of that. The reward was a choice piece of meat good enough for any restaurant in New York City. Perfect as it was, it couldn't compete with the beauty sitting across from him.

When he'd stumbled across her wandering lost in his cornfield, his first thought was she was some kind of ghost or something. It made no sense for a woman to be out there all alone, much less one in a blue party dress that fluttered dreamily with the breeze. The sun glinted off her golden hair as she turned toward the sound of his approaching horse and their gazes locked. Billy stopped breathing. She was the most beautiful creature he had ever seen. Pretty, and petite, she had her long golden locks pulled back with a blue ribbon. Her eyes, the true green of the Colorado River on a cloud-less, summer day, tore his will from him. But almost instantly, the pleading look of confusion on her face shifted to revulsion. Before he could dismount and try to assuage her concerns, she fainted dead away.

He cut a piece of the sirloin and looked up. Charlene's

shoulders were hunched up around her neck. She looked small and confused and the desire to protect her, take care of her, was so intense it startled Billy. He needed to get this woman out of here, or risk losing what was left of his shredded heart. "Do you remember how you wound up out there? Maybe you've got family nearby I should ride for. Let 'em know you're all right."

Her fork stopped halfway to her mouth. She looked up. Again, their eyes locked and Billy would've sworn he felt something physical in the gaze. Like a hand on his cheek. A brush of her lips. He swallowed and tried to push the crazy thoughts away. He didn't even know this woman, yet he could swear he'd met her before somewhere.

"You look just like him, yet the differences ... I don't know how ..." She set the fork down and cradled her head in her hands. "Tell me if you're his brother or something ... or if I've just gone crazy."

Billy put his own fork down. Contemplating things, he dragged his palm across his mouth and then scratched the stubble at his chin. The pleading, heartbroken tone in her voice tugged at him. He wanted badly to help her, but had no idea where to start. He looked at Miss Kate for suggestions. She only shrugged. All right. Billy leaned on his reason. He needed to try to understand what was in the girl's mind. "Tell me—*us* why you're so confused."

Staring at the lantern hanging over them, Charlene rubbed her temples. "Sometime today, when the sun was still up, I stood in this house, only it was rundown, practically dilapidated, and completely empty. In other words," she slammed her fist down on the table, "... old." She bounced her stare back and forth between him and Miss Kate. "By a good hundred years. I don't know if I'm dying, in a coma, or what. I've been blacking out more and more lately when he hits me ... but I've never dreamed like this."

She stopped her gaze on Billy and again he had the sensation that the look passing between them was a physical touch.

"You're so real," she whispered.

Billy had no idea what to say. *Was* she crazy? Did her husband hit her a lot? Had he beaten her to the point she'd come unhinged? On the other hand, maybe she just had a concussion. Her horse had thrown her or something.

His grandmother cleared her throat and turned a bit more toward Charlene. "Dear, you can take all the time you need to figure this out. We're not going anywhere," she reached out and tapped Billy's hand without looking at him, "and you're welcome to stay here as long as you need to. Isn't that right, Billy?"

He had to remind himself to breathe, and then he nodded. "Sure. You're more than welcome." In spite of her crazy talk, he hoped she'd stay a long time.

---

*B*illy leaned on a log post and blew a swirl of pipe smoke into the cold night air. Behind him, the door opened and Miss Kate drifted out to the porch, drawing up beside him. In thoughtful silence, they watched the fingernail moon balance for a moment on the jagged mountains opposite their valley. But, like him, she hadn't come out here to admire the night sky. He blew a smoke ring, watched it rise up and then dissipate. "What in the world do you think? I know I don't know what to think."

Miss Kate crossed her arms against the cold. "The only thing I know for sure is that girl is running from an abusive husband."

Billy's hand tightened around his pipe. "You reckon he'll

come looking for her?" He almost wished for it. Any man that would hit a woman—

"If he's lost her, yes. If he abandoned her, probably not." Miss Kate looked up at him. "You could take her in to see the marshal tomorrow. Leave her in town with Doc."

The suggestion coming from her surprised him. He straightened up and pulled the pipe from his mouth. "You'd just walk away from her?"

"I'm afraid if we don't, *you* might not be able to."

More often than not, his grandmother's wisdom was about as gentle as a sledge hammer. Billy shoved a hand in his pocket and fell back on the post again, the glow in his pipe fading some. She was right of course. The pretty little thing sleeping in their guest room was quicksand, pure and simple. He'd been running from the memory of a smiling, redheaded heartbreak for a long time now, but felt his feet slogging to a halt around Charlene.

"It's just that she strikes me as so familiar … Or maybe she just strikes me in general." He hung his head, embarrassed he was confessing any of this to his grandmother.

Miss Kate rested a hand on his shoulder. "I'd hate to see you get hurt again … and this girl …" She faded off, took her gaze back to the moon. "Probably already too late," she said somberly. "I see the way you look at her. Like your father when he looks at Hannah."

CHAPTER 3

*D*ale fluttered his eyes, then opened them all the way. The glare from the windows outlined Mimi's perfect hour glass figure. He watched with appreciation of her curves as she neatly packaged her assets back into last night's blue sequined dress.

"Good morning, Sunshine." She reached for the studded purse on the night stand. "Remember, dinner with the DNC tonight. Pick me up eight o'clock sharp."

Dale groaned and rolled over on his stomach. Every night this past week Mimi had dragged him from one fundraiser to another. Angling to be his political adviser, she was hot and heavy to get him moving in the right circles for the election in two years. Money and power. Mimi lived for it. The spicy opposite of Charlene, that was for sure …

He sat up. *Charlene.* "What day is it?"

He heard her sigh. "Friday. Do you need the date and the year, too?"

He ignored her condescending tone and threw back the sheets. His head thundered from too many vodka martinis but that wasn't his biggest problem at the moment.

21

"What's the matter?" Mimi paused in putting on her earrings. "You look like you've seen a ghost."

"Maybe," he said. Where had the week gone? He should have picked Charlene up on Tuesday. She'd been out at the ranch five days with no food, no blankets, probably no water?

He smiled at the picture that came to mind. His little wifey, weak, starving, cowering in a corner, half-frozen.

Well, she'd be a whole lot easier to get along with now, he suspected. No more of those cold stares that said he hadn't really broken her. Yes, indeed, he would break her. Just like his dad had broken his mom. Obedient wives, that's what a man needed. One to cook, clean, keep the home fires burning and the bed warm.

He was quite certain Charlene would fall into his arms and promise him anything now. No more attempts to get a job or do volunteer work. No more sneaking out for a jog or a chat with the mailman. And now he wouldn't have to resort to that other plan, the one that involved chains and handcuffs.

Charlene would finally be his sweet little Stepford wife.

Wife.

The word always made him smile. Man, he'd really pulled one over on her. Reverend Callahan was a bankrupt fake and his chapel was in foreclosure at the time. He'd conducted the ceremony for a hundred bucks and a bottle of booze.

The elaborate lie was the only way Dale could get Charlene into bed. Evaluated through a bourbon haze, the ruse had seemed like a good idea at the time. Now, with politics on the horizon, Dale had decided he and Charlene would retake their vows. She needed to be his legal wife ... or his dead wife.

*C*harlene opened her eyes and for a moment could only blink at the slanted roof, antique wall paper, and small dresser. Then she remembered. Tossing back the quilt, she disentangled herself from the sheet and hurried to the window. The towering mountains looked to be the same as those overlooking the Page ranch, but there were differences on the ground she spotted immediately.

The oak in the front yard was little more than a sapling. A hedge near the outhouse was gone altogether … or didn't exist yet. The skeletons of cornstalks waved in the distance, but this field was substantially larger than the one she'd seen on her first visit. She also noticed the barn was gone. In its place stood a long, low log structure with several windows down the side.

A man stepped out of this building, shoved a cowboy hat on his head and then started working on gloves as he ambled toward the house. Before he'd taken ten steps, another fellow emerged, hat already in place, and working his hands into his gloves as well.

Ranch hands?

Her heart racing like a spooked stallion, Charlene stepped away from the window.

Real? Is this all real?

The changes were consistent with … what the place would have looked like a hundred years ago.

Am I crazy?

She steepled her hands and pressed her finger tips to her lips. Sucking in a breath, she turned and studied the guest room. Metal-frame feather bed draped in a colorful quilt. Garish green and blue wallpaper covered in larkspurs and fern leaves. Dark knot holes in the wood floor. Simple, pine dresser. Log ceiling. All so detailed.

She sat down on the bed before her knees gave way. "Oh,

God," she whispered, with no intent to talk to him, but then she whispered it again. "Oh, God, I don't know what to think. It's crazy to think I've gone back in time." The idea of the coma came to her again. Or maybe she was dying. Maybe, like in that Ambrose Bierce story, in her final moment of life, she was dreaming up her escape from Dale ... and her death would come crashing down any moment now.

Grimacing at the thought, she rose to her feet and smoothed her night gown, a simple cotton shift loaned to her by Miss Kate. She gathered a handful of the white cotton fabric and stared at it. When she'd gone to bed last night, she'd peeled out of about fifteen different layers of clothing: a shift, camisole, lacey drawers, a petticoat, even a *corset*. She'd managed to loosen the thing on her own and was astonished at how tight it had been. How in the world had she dreamed up all these details?

Sooo ... she looked around the room again. Fine. She was not dreaming. In some crazy way, this was real. The man, Billy, was *not* Dale, but he was a Page. She was on the Page Ranch, a hundred years in the past. "God ... am I crazy?"

She waited and, in the silence, heard a faint voice whisper, *I have seen thy tears.*

I have seen thy tears?

Even though her whole life had spun out of control and nothing made sense, Charlene suddenly felt ... peaceful. That almost scared her. She'd heard drowning victims have peace at the end as they fall asleep.

She huffed, disgusted with the morose reflections. She surged to her feet again and decided to take this day one step at a time. Maybe at the end of it she would be dead. She would make the best of everything in between.

IN TIME FOR CHRISTMAS

*B*illy looked up as Charlene hesitantly stepped into the kitchen. "Hey, good mornin'," he said as he scooped an egg onto a plate. "I was just getting ready to holler at you." He motioned with the black, cast iron frying pan to a seat. "I've got coffee, eggs, hash browns, bacon, biscuits—"

Charlene tossed up a hand. "Whoa, there. You had me at coffee." He chuckled and the warmth of the sound caused a funny kind of stir in her stomach. She smiled at him and sat down. His gaze lingered for a moment. The blue in his eyes was deeper than any ocean she'd ever seen and the caramel highlights in his dark, wavy hair reminded her of molasses. He needed a haircut, but she liked the way it streamed back to his collar, mostly one length. Then he blinked and returned to the stove. "Can I help?" she asked, not used to being waited on.

"No, ma'am. You're a guest of the Box P Ranch." With skill and confidence he poured her coffee and loaded up both her plate and his with the plethora of breakfast items. Food awaiting them, he straddled the ladder back chair and grabbed a fork. "Bless this food, oh, Lord," Charlene quickly dropped her head, "and may it please get us through the day. Amen."

She muttered her own weak *amen* as well. When she looked up again, he was staring at her. The sparkle in his eyes made it hard to breathe and she was glad she hadn't pulled the corset too tight. "Do you think I'm crazy? Is that why you keep staring?"

Called on it, he jerked his gaze back to his plate and dug in. "No, ma'am. My apologies."

"No, meaning you don't think I'm crazy or that's not why you keep staring?"

He pushed the scrambled eggs around with his fork while

he thought. Finally, sounding as if the admission was pulled from him with a team of horses, he said, "I don't think you're crazy."

Charlene picked up her fork and commenced to pushing the food around on her own plate. "Thank you. I don't know what's going on–"

"But you're welcome to stay as long as you need to. Miss Kate …" He trailed off, seemed to think about something then tried again. "She said you're running from a husband who beats you. I want you to know you're safe here. I've got four ranch hands and a dog. Nobody gets by us."

To her horror, Charlene suddenly felt like crying. Her throat tightened up and tears tried to form. With a herculean effort, she blinked them back. She started to speak, wasn't sure she could, and then simply nodded. She did feel safe here but couldn't say it. Not without breaking down like a weak, emotional wreck, the kind Dale could push around, manipulate, and wield power over. The kind he had turned her into. She used to be so strong. Independent. Fearless even.

Billy cleared his throat. "Where are you from, Miss Charlene?"

She took a sip of coffee to hide her smile. *Miss* Charlene. She liked that. "Telluride." It occurred to her then that he hadn't said why he did tend to stare at her.

"Telluride's not that far. You have family over there?"

The biscuit in her mouth turned to sawdust. *Family in Telluride? Why, yes, I do. My father is a preacher there. The first and last time I ran away from Dale, I went home to Telluride. But he followed and promised if I did that again, he'd kill someone, anyone, in town … for my punishment. My dad, my mother, a random stranger. Young, old. It didn't matter. Whoever he could catch alone.*

Instead, she said simply, "Not anymore."

"That's a shame. Still, we could maybe manage a trip over there sometime. Miss Kate doesn't complain, but I know she feels a little isolated here. She's lived inside the town limits her whole life."

"Are your parents still alive?" Not the most relevant question she could ask, but Charlene couldn't help her curiosity. "I mean, how did you come to be taking care of Miss Kate."

"My parents live south of here in a town called Defiance. Pa owns a couple of mercantiles but I never really cottoned to working in a store all day. Uncle Charles, my mother's brother-in-law," he waved his fork around as he explained the family tree, "he owns a pretty big ranch there, and he let me work with him. When he bought a bigger one down in New Mexico, I took over as foreman.

"I like ranching a lot and …" He paused and Charlene got the distinct impression he was skipping over something. "Well, last year I got the bug to have my own place and get out of Defiance." He popped a piece of sausage in his mouth then tossed some salt on his eggs. He offered the shaker to Charlene, but she shook her head. If she had to guess, she would guess he was skipping over a woman.

"Miss Kate lived with us in Defiance," he went on. "She came out after my grandpa died. When I decided to take this on, she said she'd help for a while … you know, until a wife came a long." Suddenly, he seemed intensely interested in buttering a warm biscuit. As he practically buried the bread beneath a thick layer of the dairy product, he smiled and his stare drifted "Miss Kate, she's a tough old bird and adventurous. She cooks and cleans. Does all the woman's work so we can run the ranch."

Charlene almost laughed at the comment, but bit her tongue. Woman's work, eh? But Billy hadn't meant anything by it, she could tell. He was simply stating the way things were here. Dale, on the other hand, didn't care what a woman *could* do. She *would* do as ordered. In his world, that meant household chores. Period. Anything beyond that, daring to balance the checkbook, joining a gym … working as a paramedic, was punished with a good beating. She could too easily recall the pain of his fist connecting with her jaw, the burn of his foot kicking into her ribs. Swirling her fork in the grits, she asked, "Do you think a woman is capable of more than just cooking, cleaning, and having babies?"

He whistled a high-pitched tune. "I'll say." Charlene frowned at his emphatic reaction, realizing there must be quite a story behind his response. "My aunt, Naomi McIntyre, is the Cattle Queen of New Mexico now. I'll tell you about her sometime, but trust me, she's tougher than most men I know. *She's* running about four thousand head of cattle down south." He leaned forward and shot Charlene a sideways grin. "My aunt Rebecca runs a newspaper and my mother is a nurse. Trust me, the women in my family have taught me to have a healthy respect for the fairer sex."

Charlene wondered if she'd have time to hear the stories of these ladies. They sounded pretty intriguing. Based on what Dale had said about this ranch, though, Billy wasn't going to be a cattle king, or even a prince here. "I heard your family barely eked out a living on this place for over four generations. That it's not big enough for a profitable herd and too steep to farm productively."

Billy's face went slack with surprise but then a wistful, contemplative expression took over. "I don't know where to start with that." He reached up and scratched the back of his head. "Four generations?" Charlene wasn't sure if he sounded pleased or mystified. "Well, all I can say is that not every man defines profitable the same way. I want to pay my bills and be busy, but not so busy I don't have time for my family. My dad grew up without a dad and that has sort of stayed with me."

He traced a knot hole in the table, a pensive dip in his

brow lingering. "As to *eking* out a living, I'll leave behind what I can, but not so much that my kids don't have anything to work for. If they don't work for it, they won't value it. And they have to make their own choices. Take responsibility. God will either bless them or He won't."

Charlene had never stopped to think that just because a family didn't have a lot, it didn't mean they weren't happy. Happiness and satisfaction for the Page family had been defined through the lens of the twenty-first century. Who was she, or Dale, to assume the previous generations were miserable because the ranch hadn't met a materialistic definition of success? Hard work could be its own reward. She looked up at Billy and couldn't hold back a smile. "No shirkers in the Page family, huh?"

Billy's expression lightened up and he moved his hand forward, almost as if to touch Charlene's, but he smacked the table instead. "Exactly. Working hard is a ritual around here, that's for sure. Miss Kate and I won't tolerate slackers. They hit the trail pretty quick." He tilted his chair back and brought the coffee with him. "But having said that, I don't plan on standing still. I've got my eye on some parcels around me and a couple of nearby ranches. Miss Kate actually has a good head for buying land. Learned it from Grandpa. She's got some ideas for the ranch, too."

"Well, I hope you are as successful as you want to be."

He took a sip of coffee and nodded. "That's the best a man can hope for. Maybe it's not enough for the generations that come after, but that'll be for them to decide."

Charlene was impressed with Billy's wisdom. He had a peace about who he was that she'd only seen in one other man. Her father. Afraid she was staring, she changed the subject. "Where is Miss Kate, by the way?"

He chucked his thumb toward the back door. "She's out

gleaning the garden one last time. Said you could come help if you wanted to."

"I might just do that." She didn't exactly have anything else in her Google calendar.

Billy drummed his fingers on his tin mug while Charlene tasted a little bit of this and a little bit of that. He was staring again, but she decided not to mention it. Snapping himself out of it, Billy reached over to the chair on his right and came up with a dark brown cowboy hat. "Well, I guess I'd better get back at it." He donned the hat as he stood and nodded at her. He turned to go, but then paused. "One of my boys will come by around noon to pick up lunch," he said over his shoulder. "Don't let him startle you if you're in the kitchen alone."

"Thanks for the warning."

Billy licked his lips, tilted his hat back, and then did turn back to her. Squinting, looking as if he was thinking hard, he grabbed the top of the chair in front of him. "Mind if I ask you something?"

Charlene liked Billy in his cowboy hat, especially with it pushed back like that. It gave him a friendly—no—inviting look. Like he was an open book. Had no secrets. The color brought out the almost violet flecks in his irises and made his smile seem bigger, that dimple on his left cheek deeper.

His brow lifted a hair, as if he was amused by something. Was *she* staring, too? Her turn to blink. "Sure, yes, ask me anything."

"How old are you?"

The rather impertinent question surprised her, but she shrugged it off. "Twenty-seven."

"How long have you been married?"

"Two years."

"He ever cheat on you?"

"He invented the concept."

"And he beat you the whole time?"

"Only from our wedding night on. Not once while we were dating. Never even raised his voice to me."

She watched with fascination as his fingers tightened around the chair, turning his knuckles white. Did her candor surprise him or was it something else?

"Why'd you stay with him?"

She could see in his face he wasn't accusing her of anything. Or judging. He didn't assume she was in a co-dependent relationship. He didn't assume her self-esteem was so bad she couldn't believe she deserved more. All things her friends, and to an extent, her family had said. They weren't true anyway, at least not for Charlene. The truth was worse. "Because if someone has to get hurt, it's better that it's me."

Billy seemed to mull that over for several seconds. Charlene wondered if he had expected her to say she stayed with Dale because she loved him. She'd loved the man Dale pretended to be.

Billy tapped the chair with his knuckles, signaling the end of his questions. With a tip of his hat, he turned and let himself out the back door.

He left Charlene pondering the feelings she'd once had for Dale. She remembered the way her heart used to hammer when he knocked on her door or surprised her for lunch at the station. A real story teller, his jokes had kept her in stitches, and he'd never once mocked her faith. He respected that she wouldn't sleep with him until they were married. But Dale was not a Believer and Charlene's father, over iced tea in the backyard, had counseled her not to marry him. Dad had offered that advice once too often. Charlene, all of twenty-five and tired of being watched over, had let the rebel in her rear up during a particularly heated debate with her father. Next thing she knew, Dale was slipping a ring on her finger as they exchanged vows inside a Vegas chapel.

And that night, he had beaten her for poking him in the ribs while he was on the phone with a client. Charlene pinched the bridge of her nose, wishing she could block out the fists, the screaming, and the pain.

Sick of thinking about Dale, she made her way outside and spotted Miss Kate digging in the kitchen garden. On her hands and knees, she worked with determination among the dying, brittle plants, digging up beets and tossing them into the basket next to her. Though the day was a bit brisk, Miss Kate's cheeks were flushed and her strands of unruly gray hair drifted around her face. Charlene didn't have a lot of gardening under her belt—well, none really, short of caring for houseplants—but she wanted to help. She stepped to the edge of the short, white fence that protected the plot from rabbits, and waved. "Hi. I'm here to help."

Breathing hard, Miss Kate sat back and waved her over. "I'd love the extra hands." As Charlene followed the fence to the gate, the woman used the small garden claw in her hand to motion to the rows of vegetables in front of her. "I'm picking up any survivors. Beets, carrots, a few green onions. Not much left, but we don't want to waste anything. It's a final gleaning before the snow." Charlene nodded to show she was listening and let Miss Kate point her to a plant. "See if we've got any carrots worth saving ... oh, but I hate to see you work in that dress."

Miss Kate wore a serviceable, plain gray wool skirt and a thick, brown sweater. Charlene's dress was thin muslin with some pretty ornate stitching on the bodice and hem. She had no idea where it had come from, but wasn't going to hold on too tightly. It was only a dress. "It won't get that dirty. I'll be fine."

As Charlene knelt down and set to work, Miss Kate made

a few amicable remarks about the weather and the seasons in Colorado. Small talk to ease into deeper questions, Charlene assumed.

"So how do you feel today? Is your head any clearer?"

Charlene paused her fight with a stubborn carrot. *Yes, I'm even more convinced than ever that this isn't the year 2013.* Instead, she said carefully, "My head is clearer, yes."

"How are your memories? Can you recall how you came to be wandering about?"

The vivid memory of a savage punch and her head filling with atomic pain was clear as day. The wandering-in-the-cornfield part, not so much. "Honestly, I can remember some things, but not everything." True enough.

"What of your husband? Do you think he will come after you?" Charlene heard the soft smack of Miss Kate wiping dirt off her hands. "I'm sorry. Here I am just peppering you with questions. That will make your head hurt for sure."

"It's all right. I understand." The circumstances were ridiculously odd. Certainly the woman had questions. Charlene gently tugged the carrot loose, surprised by how long and healthy it was, and tossed it to the left to start a pile. "I said some pretty unusual things last night. I'd wonder about me, too."

That seemed to prompt a thoughtful silence from Miss Kate, until she said, "I said you're safe here and you are. And you're also welcome to stay as long as you need to. I ... I've been in your shoes."

Charlene exhaled, but didn't say anything. She doubted Miss Kate wanted a response.

"We should know, though, if you can tell us, will Dale come for you? And how dangerous is he?"

Charlene shook her head and rolled over on one hip so she could look at the woman. "I don't think he can find me here. And I think he's very dangerous. I would have left him.

33

Tried to once. But he threatened my family." She was surprised at herself for sharing that.

Miss Kate's hazel eye's darkened, her lips thinned into a determined line. "Well, then, perhaps that's why the Lord brought you here. We will protect you, Charlene." The woman straightened her shoulders, like a soldier coming to attention. "Your family is out of harm's way and, now, so are you."

A warmth that Charlene hadn't felt since ... since her last visit to her parents, blossomed in her heart, counterbalanced by a sad weariness in Miss Kate's expression. "Because of my husband's stubborn foolishness, I missed ten years with my son and his family. God is good, though. I got some of that time back. Hannah—my daughter-in-law, the woman my husband smeared and ran out of town—I came to know her as a wonderful woman with a big, beautiful heart. I have to say, she taught me how important it is not to judge people." Miss Kate reached down and picked up her basket. "When Billy said he was leaving Defiance, I decided to come with him because I thought I could help him get started here. Now, I think ..." she tilted her head, "maybe I'm here for you."

"I don't know what to say. You don't even know me."

"I know enough. Can you sew?"

"Pardon me?"

Miss Kate motioned for Charlene to join her. "You can't garden in that dress. I'll loan you something and we'll get started making you one more ... appropriate."

Charlene was grateful for the kindness, but her lack of any experience in a world without electricity ... well, she didn't want to embarrass herself or frustrate Miss Kate. Nervous, she climbed to her feet and tapped the carrot against her thigh. "If I stay, there's probably a lot you'll have to show me."

Miss Kate walked around a potato mound and hooked her arm through Charlene's. "I missed getting to teach Hannah anything. In fact, by the time I made it to Defiance, she was an accomplished wife." She patted Charlene's hand as they strode toward the house. "Now, I'm almost seventy-five years old. I like to feel useful. If you'll let me, I believe there might be a lot I *can* teach you."

Miss Kate smiled kindly and Charlene had the strangest sensation, like she'd known the woman for years. "I'd like that, Miss Kate. I'd like to stay until I can figure things out, and, in the meantime," she grinned at her friend, "learn how to be a good hand around here."

"Well, I reckon we've got nothing but time."

CHAPTER 4

*B*illy gazed down on his small herd, a hundred head of healthy, fat, white-faced Herefords and five sturdy, solid-black Angus bulls. A couple of the calves cavorted like children and he grinned. Three of his hands, riding well-trained cow ponies, whistled and swished their riatas back and forth, moving the cattle at a cautious, comfortable pace. Man and animals had survived their first winter reasonably well, but Billy felt a hundred percent better about this next one. Primarily because he now had some solid, experienced hands.

No, maybe this plot of dirt and his humble dream of raising up an outstanding herd of prize stock wasn't much, but it was his dream. Was that how the future generations would see this? *Eking* out a living? For someone who was eking, he was pretty content.

But the argument turned his thoughts to Charlene … again. He *had* been pretty content, until she showed up. He'd figured a woman would come into his life when the time was right. He'd meet her at church or the stockman's ball. Not wandering around in his cornfield, trying to shake a worthless husband.

Shifting in the saddle, he draped his left leg around the saddle horn and rested an elbow on the joint. He sure liked looking at her. That golden, shimmering hair reminded him of wheat swaying in a September breeze. And those eyes, green as a granny smith apple, could look right into a man's soul. She was pretty, but she was smart too. He could hear it when she talked. Even when she talked crazy. He had a feeling she was as tough as his Aunt Naomi, too.

He exhaled, disgusted with himself. He was over the moon about some little gal he didn't even know. It didn't make any sense. He'd never been one for getting rolled by his heart. He was not a skirt chaser or a shallow man. He tilted his hat back and looked at the cloudless Colorado sky. *Lord, am I in over my head? Please help me not to make a fool of myself. But if she's the one—*

"You thinking about your house guest, Boss?" His foreman, Randy Dyer, pulled his pinto up beside Billy and grinned like a horse munching on briers. "Good way to get throwed right off that horse."

Randy had helped Billy get Charlene in the house last night and, though in his forties and a confirmed bachelor, he'd been struck by the girl, too. The thought irritated Billy. "No, I wasn't. I was thinking we haven't driven this herd fast enough to the flats. We need to get a move on."

Randy stroked his bushy, pale mustache to hide a smile. That irritated Billy too. He didn't like being pegged. "We'll git'er done," his foreman promised. "Shorty is back with lunch. We'll all eat quick, get this herd off the mountain and have you back in time for dinner with the ladies."

Before Billy could reach over and punch his friend square in the face, Randy spurred his horse and loped jauntily down the hill to the herd.

Speaking of getting *throwed*, Billy was supposed to ride over to Grizzly Bear Pass. Lincoln Jones, the hermit who wandered the area, had promised the Box P an elk today for Thanksgiving. In exchange for some whiskey and new blankets.

Maybe Charlene would like to go for a ride. Maybe she would enjoy getting out of the house.

Maybe he could find his spine and ask her.

---

*B*illy ignored the tightness in Miss Kate's jaw and focused instead on Charlene's smile.

"Yes, I would like to take a ride and see your ranch …" She dipped her chin a bit out of respect toward his grandmother. "If it's all right with you, Miss Kate?"

Billy detected only the briefest hesitation before she answered. "I think you would enjoy it, Charlene." The older woman laid the bolt of cloth in her arms down on the kitchen table. "Besides, that will give me time to look for some more fabric." She pressed her index finger to her chin and frowned. "I know I've got a bolt of calico here somewhere."

On the chance that Charlene might agree, Billy had the buggy waiting. Within a few minutes they were on their way, rolling quickly through a quiet barn yard. Even the chickens were hiding somewhere.

"Where is everyone?" Charlene asked twisting her head around. "It's so quiet."

"We're moving the herd lower into the valley. Takes all the hands."

"Then why aren't you helping?"

She sounded a little suspicious of his motives. He would admit she might have reason to be. He stole a sideways peek at her. Chin raised in the air, pretty, pink lips tweaked with suspicion, she waited for the truth.

"In addition to showing you my ranch, I'm meeting someone. I have a surprise for Miss Kate." He leaned in to share the secret. "I've got a fella that's trading me those blankets in back for a big elk. *This* Thanksgiving, we're eating like kings."

"You didn't eat well last year?"

Billy steered the horses off the main drive and down a trail into the pines. He bit back the bitter laughter, but an irate huff still managed to escape. "No, we did not. We got hit with a blizzard the day before Thanksgiving. I only had two hands then. The cattle got scattered. We spent nearly twenty-four hours in the saddle rounding up those stupid creatures. Lost ten percent of my herd."

Aware he was scowling, he readjusted his hat and tried to lighten his expression. "The snow was so deep Miss Kate couldn't dig her way around outside. She tried, though. She tried digging several different paths, but finally wound up concentrating on the wood pile. When we got back she told us that, being a Southerner, she could hold out for food longer than she could for heat." He chuckled at his grandmother's pragmatic wisdom. "She's rawhide tough but the snow and the temperatures were too much for her. For Thanksgiving we ate cold biscuits and jerky. It was good and it was appreciated, but it wasn't elk or turkey stuffed with dressing."

"And what if you get hit with another storm?"

"The odds are against it." Certainly more blizzards were coming. Nothing he could do about them except be better prepared. "At least I doubt we'll get hit again on Thanksgiving. We've got enough hands to tackle any problems, though …" He grinned at her. "Including leaving someone with Miss Kate to help her get a meal on the table."

Their smiles faded awkwardly into silence as they rode.

Charlene swiveled around, taking in everything. Billy was proud of the thick stands of timber on his ranch, pastures so green in the summer the color almost hurt to look at. Water, too. He had springs, ponds, and a healthy creek that bubbled all the way through his property. Small, yes, but a good parcel and it would blend well with the property around it when he decided to expand.

Charlene nodded here and there and made breathy little sounds when she was particularly impressed with something. "It's really beautiful here." She cut her eyes at him and half-smiled. "If a person had to eke out a living, this would be the place to do it."

Billy resisted the urge to sit up a little straighter and a little taller. He had to admit it, though. What she thought about his place mattered to him. A little redhead back in Defiance had torn out his heart over this dream, or rather the fact that she didn't want anything to do with it. He really wanted Charlene to like the Box P.

He didn't want to think too hard on why.

Every once in a while the fall breeze brushed his face as they rode and he would catch the faint scent of perfume. Something sweet mixed with the clean smell of pine. He flexed his fingers on the reins, wishing he could pick up some of that glistening blonde hair hanging over her shoulder. Feel the silkiness of it in his hands ... maybe touch her cheek.

Sitting ramrod straight and staring dead ahead of them, Charlene cleared her throat. "Don't you think you should be watching where we're going?"

Startled out of his musing, he swung his head back to the front of the wagon. Had he been gaping at her like a lovesick school boy? He actually felt a rush of heat to his cheeks.

"You never did say why you keep staring at me." She

plucked at her dress as if the fabric had suddenly become fascinating.

Billy wished for a smoke. He didn't indulge but most of his hands did and it seemed a good way to look busy, buy a minute to think. Lacking the crutch, he lifted his foot to the kick board in front of them. "You're just … really …" He swallowed. What could it hurt to tell her the truth? "Pretty."

Charlene bit her lip and looked away. "Thank you."

Her deadpan response didn't sound flattered. "I'm sorry. Did I say something wrong?"

She shook her head and studied the aspen grove around them. "No. It's just that I know better than anyone else how little looks matter."

Billy stared at the horses' ears and pondered that. "You know, your husband … most men aren't like him. I think most men would rather take a beating than hit a woman."

"You're probably right. Lucky me, I picked a real winner."

"Have you let him ruin you on love then?" The question had slipped out on its own, but he didn't try to walk it back.

"I don't think so." But she dragged out the words, long and slow, as if she really wasn't sure.

Billy decided to take the comment at face value. "That's good … and this Dale." He slapped the reins to get a little more speed for a hill. "He'll get what's coming to him. Men like him always do."

Wish I could be the one to deliver it.

---

*L*incoln Jones was quite a sight. A tall, rail-thin black man wrapped in a blue and orange Indian blanket stood outside a simple shack. He wore a black, broad-brimmed hat that hid much of his face in shadows. Beneath his blanket, Charlene caught glimpses of a leather shirt and breeches. Jones' skin was tight and weathered, like a worn saddle, and an octagon-barreled rifle rested comfortably in his lean arms. Behind him, a huge elk hung from a rack, gutted and cleaned. As the wagon rolled to a stop, a huge grin opened on his face, revealing the whitest teeth Charlene had ever seen. Or perhaps they were so white because his skin was so dark?

He waved the rifle at them. "Page. Good to see you, sir. I's about to walk down the mountain and tell them Lazy J boys they could have yo' elk. But since I don't like the boys on the Lazy J, I am glad you came."

Billy smiled wryly at the old man. "I told you I'd be here today."

"White men sez things all the time. It's fifty-fifty when they be lying and when they be telling the truth."

Charlene covered her mouth to hide a smile and Billy shook his head. Setting the break, he climbed down and shook hands with the man. "Now, don't be impugning my reputation, Lincoln. I've never lied to you."

The old man snorted and then slowly rolled his dark, intense gaze over to Charlene. "Who she be?"

She heard appreciation in Lincoln's tone, but something else as well. Suspicion?

"This is our ... house guest, Charlene Williams."

Lincoln drifted up to her, his expression going slack and dreamy. "Ma'am, I knew someone like you a long time ago."

Charlene cocked her head to one side. "Someone like me?"

"A lady at the plantation. She was perty, too." He stared off at something in the past and his husky voice dropped to little more than a whisper. "She belonged ... and she didn't belong."

Do you know? She almost asked, but decided not to encourage this conversation.

As if thinking the same thing, Billy stepped up beside Lincoln. "You're talking gibberish again, Lincoln. That's no way to make a good impression on Miss Charlene."

The man slowly brought his gaze back to Billy, his eyes still glittering with a strange intensity. "You can't let her go. You gots to keep her here. You're stronger together."

"What?" Billy looked embarrassed by Lincoln's behavior and offered Charlene an apologetic shrug. "I should have warned you about him, Charlene. He's a little ..." Billy pointed his index finger at his temple and swirled it around.

Lincoln smiled at them then, clearing his expression as if coming out of a trance. "Sometimes, God has to smooth out a wrinkle. It'll be all right, sure 'nough, whichever way it goes. Is all God's will."

CHAPTER 5

*a*t dinner that night, the conversation flowed easily about ranch work and horses and cattle breeds. Billy did not mention Lincoln Jones, other than to mention the elk for Thanksgiving dinner was curing in a salt bath. Charlene had the impression he would prefer to ignore the strange old man. She, on the other hand, would ponder the interesting fellow and the cryptic comments till the cows came home.

But everything here interested her, not just the prophet hermits. Like a student starving for knowledge, she gobbled up the hints and tips Miss Kate gave her for every kitchen task. Charlene had made the biscuits *from scratch* and was quite pleased with her contribution to the meal. She'd enjoyed working alongside the older woman and she, in turn, seemed to enjoy teaching, even if she was taken aback by Charlene's ignorance. She didn't know how to light a fire in the stove, make biscuits, milk a cow, or even clean a chicken. Miss Kate had smiled that kindly smile of hers and said, "I'll handle that this evening. You can butcher him next time."

Charlene was glad. The bird's squawk, followed by a flash

of a headless body flapping around the back yard had put her heart in her throat. Killing and cleaning a chicken was definitely something to work up to. In the meantime, she was proud of herself for managing the biscuits without the help of Pillsbury.

"We lost another cow to that mountain lion."

Charlene jerked her head up. "Mountain lion?"

"Yep. Third attack this month. We're going to light a fire and double up on the watch tonight." Billy lifted a juicy fried breast from the platter Miss Kate offered and dropped it on his plate. "Tomorrow morning, I'm going to take Russell with me and hunt him down. Can't afford to lose any more stock."

Miss Kate passed Charlene the plate of fried chicken and said, "Russell was telling me he was a sniper in the Army."

Billy nodded with a mouthful of mashed potatoes. "That's why I'm taking him."

"Hunting something like that seems dangerous." Charlene plucked a leg from the tray then set it in the middle of the table. "Have you ever done it before?"

"Yes," Billy nodded then shook his head. "Well, sort of. I've hunted bear. Russell has hunted everything with four legs. I'm sure I'll learn a lot from him tomorrow."

Charlene recalled a high school athlete in Colorado Springs who had been killed by a cougar. The cat had snapped the boy's neck and dragged him off the trail better than a hundred yards. No small feat considering the victim was a defensive lineman on the varsity team. A chilling attack, the image of the partially devoured boy haunted her. The worst call she'd ever been on. She twisted her fork around in her mashed potatoes and resisted the urge to ask Billy to be careful.

"Well, be careful," Miss Kate said. "Don't take any unnecessary chances."

"I don't plan on it." Forks scraped in companionable

45

silence as the three wrapped up the meal. Billy wiped his chin and set his napkin next to his plate. "Mighty fine dinner, ladies. I am blessed and very appreciative." Miss Kate and Charlene both chuckled. "So, the boys are getting that fire started right about now. You two are welcome to come out and do a little star gazing before bedtime." The invitation was directed at both of them, but Charlene would have sworn Billy's attention lingered a bit longer on her. "Shorty said something about his fiddle."

Miss Kate picked up her empty mug. "You know, we should take some hot cider out to the boys."

"I'm sure they'd appreciate it, Miss Kate," Billy agreed with an emphatic nod.

But by the time the dishes were done and the sweet aroma of apples and cinnamon filled the kitchen, Miss Kate looked done in. Leaning over her pot of steaming cider, she rubbed her lower back and shook her head. "Charlene, this is ready to go, but why don't you and Billy take it out? I think I'm going to turn in. My lumbago is bothering me."

"Are you sure?" Charlene asked, picking up a spoon and stirring the mix.

"Oh, quite sure."

Billy strode in carrying some papers in his hand. He leaned down and kissed his grandmother on the cheek. "You're working too hard. You're right, Charlene and I can take the cider down to the boys." He winked as a smile appeared. "And these bills can wait till morning." He set them on the table then gently grabbed his grandmother's shoulders and spun her toward the door. "Scoot, my dear."

Miss Kate patted his hand and laughed softly as she glided out the door. "Don't stay up too late you two."

*B*illy gave Charlene a much-too-big-but-wonderfully-warm coat to wear down to the bonfire. She carried the mugs and he carried the coffee pot, oven mitts over both his hands. The warm glow of the fire beckoned them toward the far end of the first pasture. Shadows milled around it, some men, some cattle. "Is this a special occasion?" Charlene asked as they walked, "Or do you have a fire every night?"

Billy tilted his head and shrugged a shoulder. "I guess you could say it's a special occasion. We've gathered the herd in as close as we can and now we're counting on the fire to keep the cougar away from them tonight. We're going to take shifts on lookout and then in the morning, Russell and I are riding out."

Billy strode toward a small grouping of cows. Mooing their protests, they separated like the Red Sea on his approach. Not used to the animals, much less so many of them, Charlene looked around uneasily, half-expecting a bull to come charging out of the dark.

Several yards further on they stepped into the light of the fire. A gangly, older cowboy with a bushy, pale mustache tipped his hat at Charlene and grinned with admiration. "Ma'am." He reached for the mugs. "Here, let me help you with those." As he took them from her, his grin widened. "I'm Randy, by the way."

Before the words had left his mouth, another cowboy appeared, crowding in, causing her to step back. "And I'm Shorty." But he was really a tall, thin, bow-legged young man with shaggy red hair. His attention riveted on Charlene, he eagerly stepped between her and Billy, taking the coffee pot from the boss as he did. "Sure do appreciate you bringing us some cider."

Two more cowboys elbowed in beside him, all grins and

mustaches, and swiped mugs from Randy. "How' do, Ma'am? I'm Rusty." Rusty was short, squat, had a long beard to go with his mustache, and a moon-pie face that glowed with merriment.

"And I'm Russell." Charlene raised a brow. Russell's voice was unexpectedly deep and velvety, a pure baritone. His hair was as black as his voice was powerful. Like Billy, he had piercing blue eyes, but his were full of swagger ... like Dale's. The gentlemen eagerly passed around the mugs and poured cider into them, handing the first one to her.

"Thank you." Their eager welcome left her feeling a little overwhelmed and claustrophobic. Behind the wall of men, Billy cleared his throat. The ranch hands spread out a bit, letting him into the circle.

Frowning, Billy snatched an empty mug from Randy. "Gentlemen, may I introduce Miss Charlene Williams." Belatedly remembering their manners, each of the men removed their hats completely, bowed, muttered their greetings then heeded the disapproval on Billy's face and stepped back a bit more. "My apologies, Charlene, I didn't know I was tossing a lamb out to a pack of wolves." Properly chastised, the men moved away a little more and resumed their previous conversations.

Billy looked quite annoyed with them and Charlene looked down at her cider to hide a smile. Whether this was all a dream or ... whatever, she had to admit being admired felt nice. "I guess you don't get many women out here?" she asked, using her boot tip to worry a small rock.

"No, ma'am. And when one is as pretty as you ..." He faded off. Curious, Charlene looked up, not surprised to find him studying her with intensity. "Well, guess if I'm not careful, I'm gonna have a fight on my hands."

"Oh, I'm sure they'll behave."

"Not sure I was referring to them." Charlene's breath

caught in her throat. She wished for something clever to say but could only manage to swallow. His gaze, full of hope and a little mischief, stopped the communication from her brain to her tongue. After a moment, he sniffed and looked up at the stars. "Beautiful night."

Wishing her pulse would stop racing, she nodded. "Yes."

"Can't really see it good, though, this close to the fire."

"I guess so."

He took a sip of his cider and wiped his lip with the back of his hand. "Would you, um, would you like to walk a bit, Miss Charlene? Till you get cold?"

Somehow, she didn't think that was going to be a problem.

---

*C*harlene was nothing short of stunned. Once away from the fire, she could see the immense black velvet of the sky … and an awe-inspiring dusting of glittering, twinkling diamonds reaching to infinity. She'd looked up at the sky in Telluride and been bowled over by the heavens, but here, or perhaps the key was now, this sky was absolutely *coated* in shimmering lights. The Milky Way wound fluidly and clearly through the tapestry of stars like a mystical river. She could even make out the faint flicker of planets and swirling galaxies. She gasped as a dozen or more shooting stars shot through the sky, disappearing in a blaze of light.

Amazed, humbled, Charlene draped her hands over her heart and thought, *You are there. All this, just for us to see … and know You're there.*

Billy raised his face to the sky, but snatched several sideways peeks at Charlene. Finally, an amused smile playing on his mouth, he laughed softly. "Haven't you ever done any star gazing before?"

"Yes," she said a little breathless. "But it's all so clear here. I can see things I never could before." She realized that applied to much more than the sky. It seemed God was waving a neon sign at her. *I am here*, it said. *I am here.* And it gave her strength to wait … to hope.

"I'm a preacher's daughter." She gave Billy a moment to let that sink in then said, "When I started seeing Dale, everything else went out of my head. It was like he was an obsession or something." Billy shifted, shoved his empty hand in his pocket. She wondered if he didn't want to hear about her husband, but she needed to say this. "I put God on the backburner and drifted a little farther away from Him every day."

She bit her lip, surprised she finally had the courage to speak the truth. "When Dale started beating me, controlling me, I prayed … and prayed … and prayed." A tightness squeezed around her throat but she pushed past it. "Then I gave up. I figured the only way to survive Dale was to stop feeling. I buried everything. Anger, hurt, hope." The lump in Charlene's throat grew and she blinked back tears, pulling the coat tighter. "That," she pointed her chin at the sky, "gives me hope again. He is there and He cares about me. I feel it. I *know* it."

Billy moved towards her, hesitated, then pulled one of her hands to his chest and wrapped it in his leather-covered fingers. Charlene's heart thundered in her chest as he caressed her hand and searched her face. "He does care about you and so do—" He bit that off. As if thinking better of whatever he had started to say, he released her hand and stepped back. He stared down at the ground and massaged his neck. He mumbled something that sounded like *once bitten*. "I don't know what in the world has gotten into me."

Frustration came off him in waves. "What am I doing? I shouldn't be out here with you."

---

*B*illy didn't know a man who could read a woman's thoughts, but Charlene's face went from open and inviting, even hopeful, to disappointment in a heartbeat. Unless he was blind. He'd come so close to telling her he cared about her. Maybe he should have. Maybe she needed to hear it, but the depth of his feelings for her actually frightened him. She made him want to say all kinds of crazy things. Better yet, make him forget some things and move on.

"That is, I mean to say …" He drifted off.

He didn't know what he meant or what she needed to hear and when he didn't finish, her expression of disappointment deepened. "I can go back inside if you feel like you're baby-sitting me. Is that it?"

His mouth fell open. "You think I *don't* want you here?" Billy took another step back and clutched his cup of cider in front of him. He wasn't ready to confess to anything, but he didn't want her thinking she hadn't got his attention. Laughter from the boys drifted over to them. A reminder that he shouldn't risk being lackadaisical about her. "No, ma'am." He rested a hand on his hip and accepted this moment. "Truth is, I'm fine right where I am."

She bit her bottom lip and half-smiled. "For the first time in a long time … me too."

Billy had to consciously root his boots to the ground. That little motion, that lip biting thing she did, drove him crazy. He wanted to kiss her. He wanted to kiss her more than he wanted to run this ranch or kill that cougar. And that was precisely the reason he wasn't moving. No sir. He was going to keep his wits about him, so neither one of them got hurt. "I should take you back. I need to get the night herding squared away and make sure Russell has our supplies packed."

She nodded agreeably. "I'll go, but I can walk back alone. I can see the house from here."

"I'll keep an eye on you then." His words seemed to hang in the air, at least to him, as the statement felt loaded with meaning. He supposed it was, at that.

She licked her lips and smiled. "Well, I'll be sure to scream if I see your mountain lion."

---

*B*illy dreaded it, but after Charlene disappeared into the house, he ambled back to the fire. He knew his men were keen to do a little ribbing. If he let it get to him, there'd be no end of it, so he made a last second decision on how to handle it.

Russell was the first to have a go. "Well, boss, next time you ride out for a lost calf, I think I'll come too. Maybe I can round up a brunette."

The men roared. Billy chuckled and waited patiently for the laughter to die. "Russell, you couldn't come back with a gal that pretty if I sent you to a lady's charm school and told you to pick one out."

The ranch hands rolled, slapping their knees and ribbing Russell. He chuckled grudgingly at first then decided the joke was a good one and joined in. Beside him, Randy poured the last drop of cider into his mug then squatted to set the coffee pot on the ground. He came back up slowly, a wistful look on his face. "Russell, if you want my opinion, you'd have better luck at the charm school. That little girl don't have eyes for nobody but the boss."

The men fell silent and Billy stared into the fire. One last chance to control the ribbing. He tossed his cider into the flames. "Can't fault the girl for having good taste." The men laughed again and complained with melodramatic flare about Billy's ego. Their boss just clucked his tongue, like he was trying to move a stupid horse. "Russell, if you're done, tell me our supplies are packed."

Russell tossed back the remnants of his mug and smacked his lips with satisfaction. "Yep, I'll be waiting when you get off night herd."

"All right, well, I'm gonna go get a little shut eye then. Rusty, I'll see you for the four a.m. shift."

As Billy strode off toward the house the soft snickers followed him. He didn't mind. The boys would have their fun but they knew the way of things now. He'd more or less laid a claim to Charlene. And, if Randy could be believed, maybe she was agreeable to it.

CHAPTER 6

*I*n the two days that Billy was gone, Charlene
learned more about living without modern conve-
niences than she could have ever imagined. Every little want
or need required a humbling amount of work to achieve.
From heating the house to eating, no task was simple or
quick.

She started her days by pumping water from the well into
buckets and lugging them into the house while Miss Kate
and Randy stoked the fires in the kitchen stove and living
room. She then put a large pot of water on to boil for various
needs, like washing her hands after dumping the chamber
pots at the privy. She sliced bacon from a slab of meat the
size of a table top, collected a few eggs from the coop (Miss
Kate was not pleased with the number and commented on
the supply petering out for the winter), mixed, rolled, and cut
biscuits again, grabbed a crock of butter from the spring
house, and stirred a pot of oatmeal for what felt like an
eternity.

Sighing, Charlene blew a stray blond hair out of her face,
stared into the oatmeal and wondered when these people

rested. But it felt good to be this busy, this productive. Dale had stopped her from working as a paramedic, going to the gym, even taking walks through the neighborhood. Maybe life here was about as exciting as waiting on tables at a Waffle House, but it was ... relevant. Every chore, every task, *mattered*.

The tromp of boots interrupted her musings as the ranch hands stormed the kitchen. Amidst the good-natured joshing of men who were hungry to eat and hungry to work, she and Miss Kate set to serving food, pouring coffee, passing the butter, and frying up some more bacon. Barely taking their eyes off Charlene, the boys shoveled it all back pretty fast, nodded their thanks, and then left as fast as they'd come. Charlene blinked, astonished at the mess the hands had made. Dirty plates, cups and utensils littered the table, mud trailed across the floor, chairs sat askew. "Wow, this place looks like the mall on Christmas Eve."

A puzzled groove in her brow, Miss Kate wiped her hands on her apron. "Whatever that means." But she let an easy smile come back. "Next, it's your turn. We'll grab a bite to eat, clean up this mess, and then see if we can get started on a dress for you."

Charlene didn't really feel the need to watch what she said. Miss Kate seemed to blow off the odd slips and unfamiliar phrases. Strangely, Charlene felt more comfortable here than she did in her own time. As the two women washed dishes, she worked up the courage to ask a question that had been riding her since waking up here. "Miss Kate, what year is it?"

To her credit, the older women barely paused. She toweled off a tin plate and set it in the dish rack. "It is 1903. November 25, 1903, to be exact."

Charlene frowned as she soaped her rag and commenced to scrubbing an iron frying pan. A hundred years. She was in the past exactly 100 years. Well, give or take. Dale had abandoned her at the ranch on October 30. She'd only been here a few days. She wondered about the strange gap. Perhaps the slip in time wasn't exact. Maybe it was a wrinkle.

Ironically, though, the year reminded Charlene of a report she had written in elementary school. "In December, the Wright Brothers will fly an airplane at Kitty Hawk, North Carolina. It kicks off the aviation industry."

Miss Kate's hands froze. The woman's face hardened, as if she was troubled by something. "I don't think I'd want to know the future. A hundred years is a lot of history to see coming."

Charlene thought about that. World War 1 was on the horizon, followed by World War 2, the Depression. Images ran through head like a documentary of destruction. The atomic bomb mushrooming over Japan, the Killing Fields, the World Trade towers collapsing, Auschwitz, parents screaming and wailing over the deaths of children at Sandy Hook Elementary. She squeezed her eyes shut and shook her head. "Some of it is terrible."

The two women worked in silence for a few minutes, scrubbing, washing, and stacking dishes. Charlene sensed, though, that Miss Kate was pondering something. She wasn't surprised when the older woman said, "Tell me something wonderful, something positive that would make a person want to see the world in a hundred years."

Charlene laughed softly at the woman's curiosity. "Well, we've cured some diseases … People live longer. And indoor plumbing is certainly awesome but …" But what? How in the world could she explain the instant availability of information flooding out of the internet? Or movies and music on demand? Fast food from Chick-fil-A? Cash shooting from an ATM? Routinely driving sixty or seventy miles an hour? Posting a picture to Facebook? Checking email? Skyping?

Unexpectedly, Charlene realized that life in the twenty-first century moved like a rocket sled on rails ... and she didn't miss it. "I carry my iPhone *in my pocket* and I can call anyone I want anytime I want from almost anywhere." *And then pray Dale doesn't check my phone history.* "I own a car and can drive to a grocery store in under *five* minutes." *When he lets me.*

Miss Kate's mouth rounded into an astonished little *o*. "Oh, my," she whispered, sounding appropriately impressed.

What else? "I can walk into a room and flip a switch, and voila, lights come on. Electricity. Probably my favorite invention, next to the battery-powered toothbrush."

"Oh, I think it will be quite some time before we see electricity out this far. And those other inventions have made life so ..."

Empty, Charlene wanted to say.

"Amazing." Miss Kate shook her head. "Absolutely amazing. But tell me, what is an I phone?"

CHAPTER 7

$\mathcal{T}$eeth chattering, Charlene finished her last visit of the evening to the privy—hoping not to have to empty a chamber pot in the morning—and raced back to the fire in the living room. She warmed herself in front of the flames, rubbing her hands together. Finally ready to climb into that little narrow bed and call it a day, she slipped the screen in front of the dying fire.

"Charlene?" Miss Kate called from her room upstairs. "Could I see you for a moment?"

"Yes, Ma'am." Charlene made sure the screen was secure than hurried up the stairs. She found Miss Kate snuggled into a rocking chair, a quilt and her Bible on her lap, her lamp casting a warm, picturesque glow on the cozy rom.

Miss Kate reached for her. "Please, come and sit down. I want to share something with you." Intrigued, Charlene walked over and settled on to the little padded bench across from her friend. "I was reading and found something you might be interested in." Miss Kate dropped her gaze to the Bible and, her finger gliding along with the words, read aloud. "And Hezekiah said unto Isaiah, What shall be the sign that the LORD will heal me, and that I shall go up into the house of the LORD the third day? And Isaiah said, This sign shalt thou have of the LORD, that the LORD will do the thing that he hath spoken: Shall the shadow go forward ten degrees, or go back ten degrees? And Hezekiah answered, It is a light thing for the shadow to go down ten degrees: nay, but let the shadow return backward ten degrees." She snuck a quick glance at Charlene, but kept reading. "And Isaiah the prophet cried unto the LORD: and he brought the shadow ten degrees backward, by which it had gone down in the dial of Ahaz."

Miss Kate looked up then, but Charlene only shrugged. "I don't understand."

"God moved the sun backwards. But what He really did was turn *time* backwards. In Joshua, chapter ten, He made the sun stand still for nearly a whole day."

Charlene bit her lip and plucked some fuzz from her skirt. "So, you're saying you believe me? You're not just humoring me when you ask questions about the future?"

"I believe God still performs miracles, Charlene." She folded the book closed and stared off into space. "He orchestrates every step of our lives if we let Him." She smiled a little smile and reached over to pat Charlene's hand. "I said it before. I'll say it again. I'm glad you're here. I don't care how you got here."

You can't let her go. You gots to keep her here.

A sudden fear gripped Charlene's heart and she clutched the woman's hand. "What if I don't get to stay? I mean, what if this is just temporary? I don't know *why* I'm here. What if I don't get to stay, even if I want to?"

Miss Kate's face sagged and she nodded, as if she'd considered that possibility. "Then, as at any moment in our lives, we should make the best of it ... whether we're together or if God has some other plan." She gave Charlene's hand a firm squeeze. "He does have a plan for you, Charlene. He loves you. Do you believe that?"

He does have a plan for you. She'd only been here a few days but this ranch, Miss Kate … Billy, they felt right, familiar, like *home*. But what of her family back in Telluride? If she could find the courage to fight Dale, somehow she should be able to stop him from hurting anyone she cared about. And then she could go back to her old life. Be a paramedic again.

Was that the plan?

The thought left her a little cold. That life felt like a memory now. Her attention came back to Miss Kate and she saw where Billy got his mouth.

Billy …

"If his plan is for me to stay here, Miss Kate … I think I'd be all right with that."

*I*f Charlene had any doubts about where she wanted to spend the rest of her life, they disappeared the next morning when Russell barged through the front door, hollering for help. The commotion brought her and Miss Kate bustling from the kitchen as the ranch hand draped a very bloody and unconscious Billy on the parlor's settee. Charlene gasped and rushed to his side. The left shoulder of his coat was shredded and bloody, and his face showed the scratches and abrasions of a good fight. She pulled open his shirt and flinched at several deep puncture wounds still trickling blood.

"The cat jumped him early this morning." Russell wiped the sweat away from his upper lip and wagged his head. "I've never seen a grip like that."

"Yes, that's what cats do." Charlene's fingers drifted over the wounds. "They hold on with their claws so they can sink their fangs in ..." The image of the high school football player leaped to mind, vivid and gory. It was too easy to put Billy's face on the half-eaten corpse. She swallowed against the rising bile and forced herself to think. "Here, help me," she ordered. "Get him out of this coat. Miss Kate, could you please boil some water, bring me some clean rags, and find some whiskey?"

Her training taking over, Charlene touched Billy's neck. His pulse was weak and rapid. Clammy skin, too. His eyes flickered open. Glazed and dilated. She smiled at him. "Everything's going to be all right. You're back at the ranch." She turned her head to Russell. "He's in shock. Get me a blanket and stoke the fire."

*A*s Charlene worked on Billy, she found herself silently thanking God over and over. The injuries to his shoulder and abdomen weren't life threatening, but the cat had tried to sink his fangs into Billy's neck at least two different times. He had the scalp wounds to prove it. A little lower and a little deeper and the animal would have succeeded in snapping the spine in two.

"I've got to hand it to him," Russell said from behind her. "He fought that cat like a wild man."

Judging by the injuries, it had been a whale of a fight. The cat had had a hard time grabbing hold, which accounted for the way Billy looked. He had claw marks on his back, shoulders, forearms, and abdomen. A couple of the wounds were deep and jagged, no doubt from Billy twisting and fighting. "What happened to him? The cat, I mean."

"I tried to get off a shot but they were rolling around like two snakes. About the time I thought I was going to have to risk shooting them both, Billy managed to gut him with his knife." Russell exhaled, long and wearily. "For a minute there, I thought I might have to bring 'em both back draped over the saddle."

---

*C*harlene stitched up one last gash then sat back on her knees. Altogether, Billy had a grand total of twenty stitches. That didn't count the scores of lesser cuts and abrasions. Her hands started to shake and she put the needle and thread down on the table. She gazed down at Billy and allowed the emotions to break.

She felt sick. What if he had died? Would she want to stay here then? Maybe, but he *was* the biggest anchor tugging at her heart. Her hand, moving on its own, stroked his cheek, pushed some stray hairs off his forehead.

Russell cleared his throat. "Well, I don't think y'all need me anymore."

Charlene sensed the knowing look that passed between him and Miss Kate. She didn't care. She couldn't come right out and say she had fallen in love with Billy, but if he had died, the grief would have stunned her. She couldn't imagine going on without him. She couldn't imagine leaving him.

A hand rested lightly on her shoulder. "Dear, why don't you clean up? I'll stay with him."

Charlene shook her head. She was staying right here, bloody hands and all.

---

*B*illy was awake but not all that clear-headed when Russell, Randy, and Shorty moved him to his bed. His head hurt like he'd been stepped on by a bull, his neck and shoulders were painfully stiff, and his back hurt something fierce. Still, through the pain and the muddled thoughts, he felt her when she laid her hand on his cheek.

He knew Charlene was there. He tried to focus on the world around him, to see her face, but his eyes felt like they were going in different directions. Everything was fuzzy and his lids were so heavy. He'd try again later …

When he finally did wake, he looked right at her. Dozing like an angel in the chair next to his bed, a Bible in her lap. He wished he could reach the thick golden strands of hair trailing down her shoulder and feel the silkiness between his fingers. He gave it a try, but could only manage a gentle tug on her sleeve.

A little startled, she sat up and the Bible slipped to the floor. "Oh, I guess I dozed off." Billy weakly clutched her hand and she stared down at his fingers wrapped around hers. He half-expected her to pull away and felt some strength flow back into him when she didn't.

"I think I'll live."

She smiled and leaned closer to him. "That is the prognosis. You're pretty banged up, though. Twenty stitches. The worst suturing is in your neck and a couple in your left shoulder. You've got to be really careful not to tear those loose."

Billy was surprised by the authority in her voice. "You got the doctor up here?"

"Not exactly."

Then he knew. He remembered her hands on him, cleaning wounds, and the gentle tug of a needle. "You did it. You sewed me up."

"It's what I used to do. I was called a paramedic."

He was impressed … and couldn't help but think how handy somebody like that could be on a ranch. "You mean you're a doctor?"

"No, not exactly. I don't have quite the same background, but I'm pretty helpful in an emergency."

"I'll say. We could keep you busy around here." He tugged playfully on her hand, and she tugged back. "Lincoln was right," he said, grasping her hand more tightly. "I don't usually put much stock in his sayings, but I see it. We're stronger together."

An awkward but not unpleasant silence settled on them, the kind that was full of things to say, but no one dared. He could see the invitation, real or imagined, in her parted lips, and it made him curse these stitches. "You know what I could stand?" he asked, desperate to get his mind off kissing her. She shook her head. "Some coffee. And then maybe some eggs and toast. I'm still deciding how hungry I am."

Charlene started to pull her hand away, he held on for an instant longer then let her go. Her cheeks flushed and she rose to her feet. "I'll go get you some coffee."

"Thanks, Doc." A huge smile lit her face and he knew he'd said the right thing. Charlene was proud of her skills. As well she should be. Thank God she'd been here for him. Maybe the wounds wouldn't have killed him, but Billy suspected he was going to heal up a lot better and a lot faster than if his care had been left up to Randy or Russell.

As Charlene reached for the door, Miss Kate slowly pushed it open. Both women chuckled at the near-collision and the younger one stepped aside. "He's awake and feeling pretty good, I think."

"Like David ready to slay some more lions," he said. "Get me some coffee and I might even take on Goliath."

Miss Kate pooh-poohed his bravado with a frown and wiggle of her index finger. "Not so fast, young man" She tilted her head in the direction of the kitchen. "There's fresh coffee on the stove."

Charlene nodded and started out the door, but an unexpected stirring of uneasiness hit Billy. "Charlene?" She turned to him as she stepped through the threshold. "Don't be gone too long." Realizing his tone had sounded a bit too serious, he added, "I feel a pain coming on. I think I'm going to need my doctor." She bit her bottom lip to keep a grin at bay and disappeared down the hall. Billy stared after her until his grandmother's fitful shifting pulled him back. Her smile was light, but he saw concern in her dipped brow. "What's the matter?"

Miss Kate laced her fingers together and shook her head. "Nothing." She shrugged. "It's just the way you look at her. So much like your father."

Billy had heard the story a million times. Manipulated by his grandfather Frank Page, Billy Page Sr. had abandoned a pregnant Hannah and high-tailed it to Europe. But true love had won out. His father had said he'd never been freer or happier than when he'd bid good-bye to his family's money and gone after Hannah. They were happily married to this very day. "It turned out to be the best thing, Miss Kate."

His grandmother waved her hand and sat down in the chair next to the bed. "Oh, I know. I'll never second-guess that. And I love Hannah. I couldn't ask for a better daughter-in-law. But I find myself wondering what would have happened to Billy if he hadn't gone after her? Or if she had rejected him? I think it would have broken his spirit."

Billy crossed his arms and cocked his head questioningly at his grandmother. "Where are you going with this?"

Doubt raged in her silver-and-brown eyes. She swallowed then spoke slowly, as if measuring her words. "If she doesn't stay … I'm worried about you. If she leaves, what will you do if you can't get her back?"

Billy's shoulders sagged and he wiggled a foot fitfully beneath the quilt. "I've thought about that, too. I know she's not from here. I don't know how I know, but I do. And you're right," he looked up, "if she leaves, I don't have a clue how to go after her."

The unmistakable sound of glass shattering in the kitchen made them both jump. His grandmother launched from the chair and raced out the door in a swirl of navy blue wool. But somehow Billy knew she would only find an empty kitchen and the shards of a broken cup lying in a puddle of coffee.

He felt it. Charlene was gone.

CHAPTER 8

"**C**harlene!" The sound of Dale's angry voice slammed into her like a sledgehammer. Pain and dizziness jolted through her and her fingers went slack. The mug slipped from her grasp. She gasped, anticipating the crash. Instead, Dale thundered into the kitchen. "Charlene, what the—" The angry lines in his face deepened and he charged forward, grabbing her arm and snatching her around to look at him. "How did you do that? I was just in here." He shook her arm again without waiting for the answer. "Where were you? And why don't you look," his gaze roamed over her, "bad?"

Charlene clenched her jaw and fought the heartbreak that wanted to snatch her feet out from under her. She was back. With Dale. She imagined the sound of a prison door clanging shut. *Why, God? Why didn't You let me stay?*

Dale slapped her but her heart hurt so badly she barely felt the paltry sting. "I am talking to you."

She brushed a disheveled strand of hair off her face and looked up at him, into a face seething with fury. Charlene was stunned to realize that she *hated* Dale. Not a raging, violent, all-consuming hate like a forest fire. Just an ember, one she had been quietly nursing while denying its existence, but hate just the same. In that moment of heartbreak, the clarity of her feelings for him startled her. And if she hated him, he won after all.

"You don't even look dehydrated. Did you find some help?" He shook her back and forth, as if trying to rattle a confession from her. "Don't lie to me."

"How long, Dale?" she asked. "How long did you leave me here?"

"One week." He ground his fingers into her triceps. "Five miserable days alone and you look like you ate better than I did. Who helped you?"

"No one." She raised her chin "Just ghosts."

Dale sneered and worked his jaw back and forth, grinding his teeth. "Let's go." He shoved her toward the parlor. Charlene took two steps but turned back to the kitchen. Empty and abused by time, the room looked so desolate. The shiny ceramic and iron stove was gone with nothing to mark its life there but the piece of pipe hanging from the ceiling. The back door was missing and leaves and some small sticks had blown inside. The once pristine floor was warped and rotting. Amazingly, the stubby remnants of a few dried flowers and herbs still hung from the rafters.

*O*n the ride back to Denver, Charlene had to hold in the screams. Heartsick, she felt that God had abandoned her …yet, her soul argued that if that was true, why had He bothered to send her back to 1903 at all? Why had He given her a glimpse of another life, possibly a better one? Why would He let her feel this away about Billy if she was never going to see him again? The thought hurt, like a knife slicing into her guts. She didn't understand any of this craziness. For the first time in a long time, she wanted to pray and pray hard until God either answered her or swept her away in a flood.

"Seriously," Dale reached over and laid a hand on her thigh, "how did you survive a week in that place and look like you've been at a resort?"

Suspicious of his good humor and gentle voice, she stared out the window and watched the ponderosa pines zip by. "I don't know. I slept a lot. Dreamed a lot." The trees broke open and she could see down into Arapahoe Basin. The wide sweeping valley, surrounded by some of the tallest peaks in Colorado, lay beneath the light dusting of a fall snow. In the growing darkness, the lights of Frisco, the small town at the center of the valley, glowed and flickered invitingly.

Frisco? She'd been so lost in thought, she hadn't been paying attention where they were until now. Angry at herself for being duped again, she shot Dale an accusing look. "Frisco? We're only seventy-five miles from Denver. When you took me to the ranch, you drove all night."

Dale shrugged. "I just wanted to confuse you."

Charlene turned to the window again, seething. But now she was angry with herself for having let Dale turn her into such a brainless doormat. God had done something amazing, something utterly unexplainable and miraculous, in her life. If that didn't prove she deserved more than someone like Dale Page, then nothing did. God cared about her. If He valued her life, then so should she.

Miss Kate had said He had a plan. Charlene hung on to the hope like it was a lifeline.

"What a shame my ol' great grandpa had to go and lose his ambition. That ranch could have really been something."

Charlene turned back to Dale. "I thought you told me he

chose poor land. Land that was too steep for ranching or farming and *that's* why the ranch never succeeded."

"Nah, that's only true of the original parcel." He pulled his shades off his face and hung them on the rear view mirror. "I heard in the beginning Great Grandpa had his eye on several parcels and ranches nearby. Wanted to have five thousand acres within ten years."

Charlene was confused. She'd never heard this version of the story. Dale had told her Billy Page had been naïve about his ranching and business knowledge and completely ignorant on how to buy good land. Why had the story changed? He'd lost his *ambition?* "So what happened?"

"Ah, different stories came out of it. Too many hard winters and constant outbreaks of disease. Ranch hands that he couldn't count on. The best story, though, is what my grandpa told me. He said it was a woman that ruined Great Grandpap."

A woman? Charlene held her breath. If Dale picked up any inkling she was actually interested in this saga, he'd clam up or change the subject, just to irritate her. Relaxing, she rubbed her chin and huffed. "It's always a woman's fault."

Dale chuckled. "Maybe so. But this story was not your run-of-the-mill tale. According to Grandpa, some gal showed up out of nowhere, stayed a few days, then—poof— vanished. Great Grandpap was never the same. Lost all his *gumption*, Grandpa said. Rumors swirled among the men that he'd killed her, but nobody ever found a body."

"Killed her?"

An oily smile stretched Dale's lips and he sneered at Charlene. "Yeah, kind of have to admire him. All these years and nothing has ever been found."

CHAPTER 9

*F*eeling like she was made of glass and might shatter any moment, Charlene turned on the shower, stripped, and stepped into the warm stream. She let it flow over her, praying it would wash away all this confusion and pain.

God, I just don't understand why You performed such an amazing miracle for me ... and then didn't let me stay. I don't want to be here.

She knew what lay ahead. Walking on eggs, Dale's screaming fits, his threats, and the inevitable beatings ... imprisonment. She buckled under the weight of what a future with Dale looked like and slid to the floor of the shower. She sobbed into the water, angry with him, angry with God, angry with herself for letting Dale turn her into a simpering fool.

I don't understand, God. I've begged You to show me a way out of this marriage. Why did You give me a taste of freedom and then take it away?

And the still, soft voice whispered to her.

For My thoughts are not your thoughts,

Nor are your ways My ways ...

That pricked something in her heart and she stilled. Who was she to ask the creator of the universe why he hadn't done things her way? Charlene had expected God to perform on her schedule. Ride over the hill and save the day at the snap of her fingers. Then, disappointed He hadn't turned up, she'd turned away. Withdrawing into herself like a turtle, she leaned on the shower wall and tried to turn off her heart, her emotions, because she was more angry with God than she was Dale.

The revelation shocked her.

When had she become so petulant? So self-absorbed? So spoiled? She had stopped trusting God and now, as a result, was drowning in her misery.

I don't need to understand, do I? I just need to trust You. I've been so rebellious, Father, can You forgive me? Please, get me back to a point of trust ... of hope.

The night she went stargazing with Billy came to mind and she remembered how the diamond-studded tapestry had taken her breath away. Billy had gazed down at her with such tenderness. A glimpse of love, both earthly and heavenly? Charlene slapped her hand to her forehead and leaned back in the shower. *Oh, God, I am so stupid. So stupid and selfish.* She hugged herself and wept harder. *A miracle. You performed a miracle for me. For me. The God of the universe touched my life and all I can do is whine and complain and ask why can't You do it this way?*

What do You want from me, God? I'm yours. I trust you. With my life.

She moved to her knees and folded her hands, even as the warm water began to cool. *God, please forgive me for hating Dale. Please forgive me for not trusting that You have a plan. Please forgive me for ignoring You.* Broken, humbled, she wept and let her tears wash away the rebellion even as the sense of surrender filled up her soul. *Father, I am done with the pity-party. If You want me to stay with Dale, please make a way for me to survive it. I can't if You don't help me. But I surrender to Your will. And, please, help me forget Billy ...*

Perfect peace. Perfect peace and love wrapped around her like a warm, soft blanket.

I have heard thy prayer, I have seen thy tears: behold, I will heal thee ...

And she believed.

CHAPTER 10

*D*ale wasn't stupid. He was furious Charlene thought she could get away with this. Who had met her up that that ranch? The mailman? Her calm denials hadn't convinced him she'd been alone.

Dale was in and out over the next several days. He acted the same, but Charlene saw a difference in the way he looked at her, with suspicion, possibly even fear. Like a wild animal, fear might cause him to lash out with less reason and more viciousness. But what was he afraid of? Did he sense her peace?

Just before Thanksgiving he told her he was going on a business trip to Seattle and would be gone over the holiday. Sounding almost weary, he stared into the fridge and said, "I'll be gone a week. Stay here. If you leave, I'll know it. If you call anybody, I'll know it. Understand?"

Charlene had been reading her Bible and committing scriptures to memory. She hadn't bothered with that since college. Now, the words rushed at her and gave her peace. *You are my hiding place;* she recited mentally as she pulled a casserole from the oven. *You shall preserve me from trouble; You shall surround me with songs of deliverance.* "I understand, Dale."

He watched her as she finished dinner. His cold stare drilled into her. Things had changed between them. Several times since he'd brought her home he had lost his temper and raised his hand to her, but instead of striking, he'd walked out of the room. Charlene didn't question the changes. She felt God's protection, yes, but she also felt as though she was waiting. On what? A big blow-up? A major beating? An announcement? Was Dale going to leave her? She knew about the woman he was taking with him to Seattle. He wasn't exactly discreet on the phone.

He grabbed a Heineken and shut the refrigerator. "I'll be back Sunday night." He lifted his chin and scowled, challenging her to say anything. "Late."

"Fine." Charlene loaded his plate with the ham casserole and set it on the bar for him. "I'll save you some turkey." He didn't return her thin but sincere smile.

The morning Dale left, Charlene spent some time in prayer. While her heart still wanted out of the marriage and she pined for a man long dead, she accepted things and waited on the Lord. *But what am I waiting on?*

As if in answer, the urge to call home hit her clear and hard. But Dale would know. He checked her phone constantly.

So be it.

"Hello?"
   "Hey, Mama. Whacha doing?"

Her mother's slight, delicate laughter. "Charlene! How nice to know you're still alive."

"I know, I know." The women chuckled together over the old joke. "We've just been busy. How are things? How's Daddy?"

"You're father's good. He's away right now, up on the Crow Reservation doing some missionary work. But he'll be home in time for Thanksgiving."

Amazing how her mother could wring an accusation and an invitation out of the same words. "If I could come, I would … I miss you."

Perhaps Charlene had sounded too honest because it took her mother a few seconds to respond. "Charlene, I've been praying for you. I mean, more than normal. Is everything all right? Are you and Dale doing okay?"

"Yeah, we're fine." The cheer in her voice sounded forced. "We're actually kind of in a good place right now." And that was true. He hadn't hit her in weeks.

"That's good." More silence, then her mother said, "Glenn won the election. He's our new marshal."

Technically, he was the new *Chief*, but it was nice to hear. Glenn Millheiser was an old friend from high school. They had stayed in touch over the years, even after Charlene had moved to Denver. Nothing romantic, just friends. Of course, because of Dale, she hadn't talked to her old friend in two years now. "Tell him I said congratulations. I'm sure he'll be a great law man. It's what he's wanted all his life."

Her mom then caught her up on the latest happenings in Telluride, what celebrities came in for this or that festival, how church attendance was, the weather report, her hip problems, a new meatloaf recipe. Charlene smiled at the deluge of information. It was so good to hear her voice.

"Mom," she interrupted her mother in mid-sentence, "if

there is any way I can get there for Thanksgiving or Christmas, I will."

"Oh," her mother sounded surprised. "Well, we'd love to have you. You haven't been home for either in two years."

They chatted another few minutes and by the time they hung up, Charlene felt an unexplainable stirring of hope, but she still had no plan, no next step. She was waiting on something. Shrugging, she decided to get the Christmas decorations down from the attic. Only strangers would see them from the street. No one would come in and see the tree or stop by for cider. Dale wouldn't allow it, but still her spirit was light … lighter than it had been in a long time. It had snowed overnight, she had hot chocolate in her hand, and her parents were all right. Dale most likely would beat her if he found out she had called home without him in the room, but it would be worth it.

*C*harlene and Dale shared an old Victorian home in Sunnyside. He had bought the narrow, three-story house because this was *the* up-and-coming neighborhood in Denver. Charlene did not care for three stories, but Dale did not care for her opinion.

Accepting the climb, she trudged her way up to the third floor, yanked open the stubborn attic door, and looked up the dark, narrow staircase. It tended to be a bit of a feat navigating the stairs, especially with anything in her arms, but she squared her shoulders and proceeded to climb.

Brrrr.

She tried to shake off the cold in the attic as she reached for the overhead light at the top of the stairs. It weakly illuminated a haphazardly arranged assortment of cardboard boxes, an old vanity, a dress form, and several Rubber Maid tubs. So where were the Christmas decorations …?

Tossing mental dice, she shrugged and started searching in the corner on the right. She slid a stack of bright orange tubs out of the way, but paused when she saw the antique trunk and cardboard boxes behind them.

Dale's father's belongings.

The elegant steamer trunk called to her and she eagerly shoved the Halloween decorations out of the way. Enthralled by its age and mystery, she lovingly ran her hand over the leather bands and metal corners. The size of a small elephant, it was made of walnut, didn't have any stickers on it, and was pretty scuffed up.

Oh, she loved these old things.

Carefully, she flipped the rusty metal latch and pulled the trunk open, marveling over the ingenious use of space. One side was a mini-wardrobe and it still had a few wooden hangers and a moth-eaten gray suit hanging on one. Someone had tossed in a couple of pairs of shoes at the bottom and a bowling ball in its case. The other side was a mini-dresser consisting of four drawers adorned with rusty, ornate metal handles.

She pulled the drawers out one by one. The first one was filled with some old shirts and an expensive pair of wing tips. The second and third drawers were a mix of clothes, a couple of football trophies, Grandpa Roy's framed high school diploma, but the bottom drawer … when Charlene pulled it open she sucked in a breath.

A leather book with the words Photo Album embossed on the cover peeked up at her. She wiggled the drawer all the way out and slowly picked up the book. The leather was dry and cracking in places on the cover and on the spine. The ties on the open side disintegrated in her hand. She ran her fingers over the edges of the pages, some of the brittle paper flaking off.

The attic was no place to examine the photos so she hugged the book to her chest and rushed back downstairs to the warmth of the kitchen. A few minutes later, another cup of hot chocolate in hand, she settled at the bar and started carefully flipping pages. The first photo was of a young couple in nineteenth century garb, with a child, maybe two years old, standing in front of the Page & Co Mercantile. Charlene suspected the store was new and this was a grand opening moment. The man was clearly a relative of Dale's. She could see the similarities in the features. But the boy ... was that Billy? The eyes and the mischievous grin were familiar, but time had started its march across the paper. Chemical breakdown and poor storage made the facial details indistinct and splotchy.

With every page she turned, she prayed for a picture of Billy, but wondered at the same time if she was just torturing herself. She saw several photographs of the young woman from the first page. Charlene came across one of this girl and two other women, taken at a picnic perhaps? It was hard to tell, as the edges of the photo had faded substantially and the paper itself was flaking and creasing, erasing crucial details. Charlene could make out, though, three women, two fair and petite, the third dark-haired and taller, seated on a blanket, surrounded by plates. Still, family similarities were clear. Sisters? They stared at the camera with ridiculously serious expressions, as if smiling would cause a scandal. At the bottom, someone had written *Hannah, Naomi, Rebecca*.

Billy's Aunts?

Charlene's breath caught when she found what she was looking for on the next page. A photo of Billy and Miss Kate standing on the porch of his new ranch. Black speckles invaded the photo, and the bottom right was turning a dark silver and beginning to flake off, but she could see Billy's face well enough. He was as handsome as she remembered. Piercing silver eyes stared back at her, that ridiculous cowboy hat sat tipped back on his head, and shadows highlighted his square jaw. One hand rested casually on the gun at his hip. A serious expression on his face, he looked like the proverbial lord of the manor.

Miss Kate, her hair pulled back in a loose bun, also wore a stern expression for the camera. A dishtowel rested over one shoulder and she held a wooden spoon in her right hand. Charlene had trouble reconciling these somber strangers with the warm, friendly people she knew them to be. Beneath the pair, someone had written the letter P then drawn a box around it, followed by the word *ranch* and *1902.* She sagged a little as she stared at Billy's face. Despite his serious countenance, Charlene could see the pride. He loved that ranch.

The next page had a few pictures of his crew. Though this photo was old and fading as well, she still recognized Randy, Shorty, Russell, and Rusty, leaning casually on each other. The second photo was also a group shot. In this one, the men looked cleaned up and shaved, stood straighter, and wore—she squinted and leaned closer—string ties and polished boots. A few of the faces were faded beyond recognition, but she could make out Russell. He was posed like Wild Bill Hickok, wearing fringed leather clothing, proudly holding a long rifle by his side, staring off into the distance, as if he was looking for bandits. The picture seemed rather formal, based on what she knew about this group. Had it been taken for a special occasion?

A party?

They probably had parties at the ranch or went to parties at other ranches. Billy most likely met his wife at some square dance or stockman's ball or whatever they called them. Or maybe he met her at a church social. Either way, Charlene hoped he had found love and was happy and the nonsense about him losing his ambition was just that. Nonsense. Billy wasn't the sort to be laid waste by a woman. He had dreams for that ranch.

Wondering why he wasn't in this particular picture, though, she slowly flipped to the last page.

And in this final photo, Billy stared back at her. Only, he was holding the hands of his bride.

CHAPTER 11

*B*illy's wedding photo, sadly, was the most damaged of the whole album. Though his face was intact, most of the picture had succumbed to a gray veil that threatened to darken the whole picture. Charlene could see his face, though, and those blue eyes well enough, hauntingly silver in the photo …

At first, the face of the bride didn't register with Charlene, obscured as it was by the damage and a hairdo that swept the girl's hair up into a loose bun. But something about her …

Charlene peered closer …

Scrambling like someone had dropped a snake in her lap, Charlene launched back from the bar and slammed into the wall. She shook her head back and forth, sure her galloping heart was about to explode in her chest. *Is that me?*

She stood stock still and stared at the album on the bar for what felt like forever. *Is it? Or am I seeing what I want to see?*

What if it's not me?

What if it is?

Gradually, as if she was approaching a wounded animal, Charlene inched her way back to the photo. She studied every shadow and crease and feature. Apparently taken in a studio, she could make out a faint pair of Greek columns that framed the couple. Billy and the woman were holding hands, showing off their gold bands. He wore a three-piece suit, polished boots, and his cowboy hat. *Even in the wedding picture.* She smiled and lightly stroked his face, missing him so much it hurt.

The right side of the photo had been substantially damaged, perhaps because that was the side of the book open to the air. What wasn't creased was turning black or flaking. The wedding dress had an A-line skirt with a bustle, both covered in lace and pearls. Charlene could discern a mutton sleeve, but the image had flaked in a few important places and was growing so dark in others the detail was disappearing. Part of the woman's cheek had disappeared, leaving only the other side of the face intact, but dark. Charlene stared and stared, but she just couldn't be sure.

Huffing in exasperation, she paced the kitchen floor. *Oh, Lord, what am I supposed to do?* Feeling undone, incomplete, she flipped back to the photo of Billy standing on the front porch of his home. She longed for him, wanted to be with him with a yearning that took her breath away. He felt so right, so familiar, as if she'd known him her whole life. It didn't make any sense. And what if she could make it back somehow? It would cost her everything ...

Trust in the Lord with all thine heart and lean not unto thine own understanding ...

That wasn't exactly an answer ... but she felt the wisp of a plan forming and understood she had to take a step out in faith.

"*M*om?"

"Charlene?" Her mother was surprised to hear from her again so soon. "Is something wrong?"

"Mom … I need you to come get me."

"I'll try to be there before dark."

Charlene smiled and hung up the phone. She knew her mother wouldn't question or whine. She wouldn't waste time asking for an explanation. Her daughter needed her and she would come running, no matter that Telluride was nearly six hours out of Denver. It wouldn't matter if it was *sixty*. In the meantime, Charlene had a letter to write.

------

*L*inda Williams' Land Cruiser pulled into Charlene's drive way at 5:00 p.m. on the dot. The car door opened and Charlene rushed outside to hug her mom. Only, it was her father Nathan climbing out of the truck, a big bear of a man wearing a sheepskin coat. "Dad!"

Charlene danced through the ankle-deep snow and dove into her father's waiting arms. "Pumpkin," he said, spinning her around. "It's been too long!"

"I know, Dad, I'm sorry."

He gave her one last squeeze then set her down. "Give Mama a hug." Charlene realized her mother was standing at the hood watching them and squealed. "Mom!" Linda, wearing a smile as bright as the red curls poking out from under her knit hat, opened her arms. The two women embraced.

"Honey, we sure have missed you." Her mother pressed her cheek to Charlene's and sighed. *We love you. We miss you. We're here for you.* That sigh said it all. "Now, tell us what's wrong and how we can help."

"My bag's at the door." She pulled away from her mom. "Let me get it and I'll be ready to leave."

Linda and Nathan glanced at each other, perhaps puzzled by their daughter's sudden, all-fired hurry to get out of Denver. "All right, sweetheart," Linda said nodding, "Whatever you say."

*C*harlene sat in the back seat studying her parents' profiles. Her mother's pert little nose and curly, rusty hair made her look younger than sixty-seven. Her dad, a big man with broad shoulders, overpowered the front of the Land Cruiser, especially in that thick coat. He had a square jaw that was straight and true like his heart, and thick silver hair that he swept back to his collar.

She met his eyes in the rear view mirror and saw his concern.

"You were right, Dad, you know. I shouldn't have married him." He shifted back to the road and, mercifully, didn't respond. "He's abusive." Her mother stiffened, but held her peace. "And he's cheated on me regularly."

Linda reached over and grasped her husband's hand on the gear shift, as if for confirmation. "We've known something was wrong for a while, but the urge to pray for you over the last month has been so insistent." She turned in her seat so she could see her daughter. "Are you leaving him?"

Charlene's mouth went dry. She didn't know where her parents were going to come down on this, her father being a preacher and all. Divorce wasn't a popular option. "Yes."

Nathan exhaled a sound that was something like a sigh and a growl. "God hates divorce. I try to get my people to go to counseling but when abuse is involved, I suggest counseling *and* a separation." He lifted his gaze to the mirror again, "Honestly, though, when it's my own daughter ... I'd just as soon shoot him."

That pretzel knot tried to come back to Charlene's throat. 'You'd do anything to keep me safe, wouldn't you, Dad?"

"You know it."

She blinked back tears as she thought about how much she loved her parents. Which was why she had to protect them. "There's something else." She leaned forward and rested her hands on each of their seats. As the SUV followed the rising road, leaving Denver behind and headed for the mountains, Charlene's sense of peace grew. She knew she could finally tell them everything. Still, she lowered her voice, as if Dale might hear. "I haven't come home in two years because Dale threatened to hurt you." Her mother gasped and an angry flush rushed up her father's cheeks. "Maybe I should have told you, but he said if I ran away from him again, he'd kill you ... or some random person from town. I couldn't risk that."

"We have to do something," her mother sounded shocked, panicked. "He can't get away with that."

"He won't get away with it." Nathan's hands choked the steering wheel and Charlene wondered if he had them around Dale's neck. "We'll talk to the law."

"I already have. There's nothing they can do. Dale is a lawyer. He knows exactly how far he can go." They rode in silence then for a long while, mulling over the options. There didn't look to be any way out of this mess. At least not one that would make everybody happy. So she had to protect her family. "If I was gone, and you didn't know where I was, he wouldn't have any reason to hurt you." The pain in her parents' eyes was more than she could bear and she fell back against the seat. A shroud of silence pulled them closer than they had been in a long time. The sun slipped behind Topeka

Point and Charlene hugged herself, praying she was doing the right thing.

"How do we convince him we don't know where you are?" Her mother rubbed her temple. It had been a long day for her. "Why should he believe us?"

"I have to convince him I'm going somewhere he can't reach me ... and that I'm never coming back."

She knew that hurt her parents. It hurt her. "Do you think you can get word to us?" her father asked, sounding a little strained. "You know, when you're settled? If it's safe."

Somehow, some way, she would. "Yes, Daddy."

*harlene slept in her old twin bed that night and rested with more peace than she'd had in two years. She shared coffee and a devotion with her parents the next morning, helped her mom cook a big breakfast then went shopping with her for all the Thanksgiving fixings. She didn't think she should hang around in Telluride too long, but she wanted one last glimpse of home before ...

The nagging worry that Dale might somehow surprise her wouldn't let up. Expecting him and being ready for him weren't the same things. There was no room for error. After she helped put the groceries away, Charlene borrowed the SUV and headed back into Telluride.

A picturesque ski town full of old Victorian buildings, it still had the flavor of the Wild West and brought in tourists year-round. But with snow on the ground, visitors were here now solely for the powder. Sitting at a stop light, she admired the Sheridan Hotel. Built in 1895, the well-preserved, red brick building had survived floods and fires and fights. In the early days, rowdy miners used to stay there when they struck it rich. She wondered what they'd think about the hot tubs on the roof.

Chuckling, she grabbed her iPhone from the console and dialed an old friend.

"Yeah, Chief Millheiser here."

His no non-sense tone caught her off guard and Charlene had to stifle a giggle. "Good morning, Chief Millheiser. This is Charlene Williams."

"Charlene?" He sounded genuinely happy and surprised. "Hey! It's been too long. Are you in town?"

"Actually, I am and I was wondering if I could round you up for a congratulatory cup of coffee?"

"You are in luck. I am parking as we speak. I'm at Between the Covers. Large coffee?"

"If you wouldn't mind, sir. I'll park and meet you at the bench in front of Silver Star Rentals. It's still there, right?"

"It's still there. See ya in a few."

hief Millheiser, dressed in his official marshal's coat and the department's black ball cap, waved a cup of coffee at Charlene as he hurried down the side walk. An eager deputy most of his adult life, she was glad he was finally chief, but law enforcement was putting a few years on him. Only four years older than she was, the crow's feet at his eyes were more pronounced and she saw a few gray hairs mixed in with the brunette. But she could still see shades of the boy from high school.

She rose to meet him and he smiled down at her. "Great to see you, kiddo." He bent and kissed her on the cheek, no small move since he was a good six-and-a-half feet tall and towered over her small frame. "We've missed you around here."

She took the coffee and they sat down on the bench. "Yeah, I wish I'd never moved away, but it is what it is."

"Yeah, I guess so." He sounded a little puzzled as he settled down beside her. "How long are you in town?"

"Not long. Not long at all." She pulled her gaze away from the busy main street and looked at him. "Congratulations on the election. You'll be marshal a long time."

"Oh, I don't know about that. There's already more politics involved than I like." She nodded, took a sip of the coffee, and stared at her boots for too long. Glenn elbowed her lightly in the ribs. "You gonna tell me what's wrong?"

"What makes you think anything is wrong?"

He shook his head and laughed like she was really entertaining. "Just 'fess up. Your face is a neon sign. Always has been."

Busted. "OK, fine. I came here because I left my husband." She looked down again at the Styrofoam cup in her hands so she wouldn't have to see the pity in his eyes.

"And …" he coaxed.

"And he said he'd hurt someone in my family or just a random person in town if I left him. I wanted to warn you."

Glenn's smiled turned into a shocked *o* and he sucked in a breath as he thought. "That's … that's, um … bad." He scratched the back of his head then removed and readjusted his cap. "OK, so, has he done anything actionable? Do you have a restraining order or anything on him?"

"No, he's a lawyer, so he's covered all his bases. But I have this …" She pulled an envelope out of her pocket. "I wrote down the details for every time he's ever hit me, every threat that I could remember, every person he's ever mentioned that he didn't like in Telluride … including you," she added with a smirk. She put it in his free hand and closed his fingers around it. "I know this is vague, but if anything happens to Mom or Dad, or something happens to someone in town, I just wanted you to know about him."

"Um, OK …" Glenn looked at the envelope and his shoulders dropped. "This is one of those things that makes me feel so helpless and stupid. Hemmed in by the law rather than freed by it." He turned more fully to Charlene. "How dangerous is this guy?"

Charlene touched his cheek, moved by his concern. It felt so good to be back among friends, to have what she was saying valued, trusted. "He's capable, but I'm leaving town. I hope to convince him that … he can't follow me where I'm going and he can't ever get me back. Maybe then he'll give up."

Glenn scrunched up his face in disgust and leaned back on the bench. He spread his arms over the back of it and looked up through the barren branches of an old elm. "Your mom and dad practically raised me, Charlene. You know that. I think the world of them." He stared at the canopy overhead for several more seconds then slowly cut his eyes over at her. "Give me a description of Dale. I'll handle him … with or without the law."

*C*harlene and her parents bustled around cooking up their Thanksgiving feast, the mood light and festive. Doubts hounded her, though, especially as she watched her parents together. Mom, in her favorite copper-colored sweater, and Dad in his loud, western shirt. The couple laughed and mixed up a sweet potato pie together like two lovesick teenagers.

What if she'd made the wrong move? What if Dale showed up and hurt them? And what if the final part of this plan was hers and not God's?

Oh, God, please don't let this be a mistake.

Perfect love casteth out fear.

Ok, ok. I'll quit doubting ... or at least I'll try to. You've got a plan. Please help me follow it to the letter.

She paused in her task of setting croissants on a baking sheet and walked over to hug her parents. "I'm so glad I'm here. You can't imagine how I've missed you."

Nathan and Linda leaned their heads into her and patted her hands on their shoulders. "Oh, yes we can," her mother whispered.

Later, when the house filled with cousins and aunts and neighbors and friends from church, Charlene slipped out to the front porch and gazed up at the slopes in the distance. Skiers couldn't have asked for a more glorious Thanksgiving Day. Temps in the low twenties, a fresh snow overnight, blue sky overhead. She squinted to make out the dark spots moving down the mountain and envied how many of those people didn't have a care in the world. At least not for the ten or so minutes they spent shushing down the mountain.

She wondered about the Thanksgiving she'd missed at Billy's. Did the elk turnout? And what of the pie she had started with Miss Kate ...?

A hand landed lightly on her shoulder as her father stepped up beside her. "When are you leaving?"

They both stared out at the slopes. "In a little while."

"What? So soon?"

"I'm afraid Dale is going to show up."

"We can handle him."

Charlene put her arm around her father's substantial frame and leaned her head on his shoulder. "It's not really you that I'm worried about, or even Mom. I'm afraid he meant it when he said he might hurt some random stranger." Nathan kissed the top of her head and Charlene wished she could cry in her daddy's arms one last time. But she would be strong for him. "If he took a jogger off a trail or, I don't know, hurt a child, I wouldn't be able to bear it."

"All right." He stroked her hair. "I've been praying and I'm with you on this." He kissed the top her head again. "It's not what I want, but it's not my job to worry about what I want."

Charlene chuckled and thought about her plan. "Dad, when did you say your family came West?"

"Uh, your great-great grandparents moved out here in 1854."

"Did they ever go home after that, or see their parents again?"

His hesitation answered the question.

"Why did they leave?" she asked.

"Well, near as I can recall being told anything about it, *he* wanted to settle a country. *She* wanted to settle him. She loved him enough to face blizzards, droughts and Indian attacks ... without turning back."

"Think she ever regretted leaving ..." Where was it? "Georgia?"

"Most likely she had her moments. But while we are called to honor our parents, Charlene, we are also called to start our own families. It's the way of things. Sometimes, that means you pack up your tent and head out ... and special people get left behind."

She saw Billy's face and hoped her feelings weren't some delusion. And that he felt the same way. "I guess."

"Look, I better get back inside." His voice sounded strained and she looked up. "Don't stay out here too long and catch a chill."

The pain in her father's eyes was wrenching. Charlene drifted her hand across his as he turned. "I won't. I just need to make a quick phone call."

She waited for the door to shut then pulled her phone out

of her vest pocket. Wishing for some chap stick, she dialed Dale's number.

"Yeah?"

Charlene's breath caught in her chest and she prayed for strength. "Dale, I'm leaving you. In fact, I'm already gone." *No sense in beating around the bush.*

She waited for his response, letting the silence go as long as it needed to. Finally, he said, "And, what? You think I can't find you?"

The mutter of a crowd in the background and the rattle of dishes clued her in that Dale was sitting in a restaurant somewhere. She hoped the setting would keep him calm, or at least restrain him. "Dale, please just make this simple. I'm going to disappear. My parents do not know where I'm going. Leave them alone. Leave me alone."

"You remember what I said I'd do if you tried to leave me again? Why would you want to bring down that kind of trouble on your parents … or some single mom who doesn't have anything but a waitressing job at the Chop House?"

The example was so specific it made her palms sweat, despite the cold air. "Dale, I'm not kidding. Where I'm going, you can't follow me, you can't get me back."

Again, a long silence before he answered. "There is no such place." And he hung up.

CHAPTER 12

*D*ale tipped his Chop House waitress, a very talkative single mom, with a $20 bill then wandered back out to Main Street. He dodged a set of skis as a powder bunny swung them around to talk to her friend. Dale almost lit into her, but a passing cop car stopped him.

Telluride Marshal's Office. How very ... western.

He pulled out his iPhone and shielded it from the afternoon glare. He quickly swiped screens with his thumb looking for an app. Seconds later, he had located Charlene's phone and smiled. "Thank you, Steve Jobs." Humming a merry tune, he headed for the rental car.

*C*harlene stared at the dark screen on her phone. Fear slithered up her spine. No, it wasn't fear exactly. It was ... an urgency ... to get out of Telluride. Dale was coming. Maybe he was already here. She ran a cold hand through her hair then brought it back around to her mouth, curled up into a fist.

Time to go, Charlene.

Doubts clawed at her. If this worked, solely by the grace of God, she'd never see her parents again. She only hoped that wouldn't be because Dale had killed her. She squared her shoulders and marched back into the house.

As discreetly as possible, she herded her parents into the kitchen. "It's time for me to go." Their mouths fell open.

"Please, Charlene," her mother touched her arm, "there's got to be a better way."

"I don't think there is. But I'll get word to you." She squeezed her hand. Hard. "Somehow. When I'm settled."

"Do you think you might ever ... come back?" Nathan waited for an honest answer, but every muscle in his weathered face said he didn't really want one.

"Anything is possible, Dad."

---

*S*he was just twenty-seven-years-old. And her parents' only child. Strangling the steering wheel of their SUV, she forced herself to look up at them. Standing on the porch, arms around each other, they offered a wave and a nod. The SUV of another guest pulled up beside her, blocking her view. Milton Barwell, an attorney in town since forever, waved a greeting at Charlene. Half-heartedly, she waved back.

She sighed at the blunt ending to her good-bye. This wasn't fair to them. And it was horribly cruel.

It was also the only way to keep them safe.

She jammed the key into the ignition, cranked the truck and backed out of the driveway before they saw her cry.

---

*D*ale had been prepared to sit in his rental car till the wee, small hours of night, when the last light died in this nice little neighborhood of hundred year-old Victorians. He was tickled pink, then, when Charlene didn't make him wait. She jumped in the Land Cruiser and took off … alone.

Dale picked up his binoculars. The devastated looks on Nathan and Linda's faces hinted strongly that she was leaving for good. Delighted, he tossed the binoculars to the passenger seat and slowly pulled out from behind a pile of snow. Slipping on his sunglasses, he followed his wife at a safe distance. When she headed south out of town, he thought maybe he knew where she was going and wondered if he could be so lucky. Settling into his seat for a three hour drive, he flipped the radio on and, amused by the irony, helped George Strait sing about murder on music row.

*W*hen Charlene passed the sign for Norwood, the last dot on the map closest to her destination, she held her breath and looked around at the mountainous, snow-covered terrain. Nothing looked familiar, but it *felt* right. Monotone Siri spewed mindless directions based on the GPS coordinates. Charlene would follow the robotic voice until the signal died.

Nine miles later, Siri stopped talking. Another mile on, Charlene turned right on Bohannon Road, or that was her best guess. The wooden sign was old and faded. The snow changed the look of everything and she prayed she was going in the right direction. The county had not scraped this road and the snow was a good eight inches deep here. Eventually, the grade on the road and ever-deepening snow proved too steep for the Land Cruiser and she pulled over.

Charlene got out of the SUV, shoved her hands into her vest pockets and studied the landscape. The road continued up at a steep angle from the base of a mountain. This mountain rose high and hard on the left, and on the right a creek trickled by. That looked right.

"OK, God," she whispered. "Almost there."

She reached inside the truck for her down jacket and bed roll and started the hike.

This time, Dale was prepared for the elements. He parked behind Charlene's truck, laced the top of his Sorel boots and slipped into a thick down coat. Stepping out of the Subaru, he breathed in the cold, crisp air and grinned. He felt good. He could do this. No witnesses. A remote area. It would be months before anyone found her and, by then, Dale would have an ironclad alibi in place. The sun was just about to slip behind the western ridge and he cursed her for making him finish this in the dark. Worse, he'd have to scramble back down that rough, snow-covered road with nothing but a pen light.

He spotted her tracks in the virgin snow. At least this part would be easy. A blind man could follow them. Feeling like a mountain lion stalking an unsuspecting deer, Dale started on the hunt for his lovely wife.

Charlene opened the door into the front parlor and her heart pinched at the sight of peeling wallpaper, the rotting floor, a crumbling fireplace. How she longed to see Miss Kate's Victorian furnishings and a cozy fire burning in that fireplace … and Billy walking out of the kitchen, something real and everlasting in his eyes.

"Well, God, I'm here," she whispered to the forlorn and empty room. It felt like home, even in this condition. The Box P Ranch felt good and familiar. "Now what?"

A chill hit her and Charlene realized she'd best build a fire and peel off some of these sweaty clothes before the moisture cooled her down. She'd gotten pretty good at fire duty for Miss Kate and had a decent blaze going in a matter of minutes. Most of the glass was missing from the front window, so the room wouldn't get warm, but she could stay next to the fire.

Cross-legged, she sat on a wool blanket and stared into the flames. She expected Dale would be along anytime now. For once, she'd used his own tricks against him and tracked his phone before she'd left her parents' house. She'd only been a little surprised to learn he was *in* Telluride rather than on his way there.

Panic tried to slither icy hands around her heart as she thought about the danger she'd put herself in. She shook her head. *No, I'm not afraid. God has a plan. I'm here for a reason. I believe that. Oh, God, please don't let me die tonight … unless it's the only way back.*

CHAPTER 13

*S*till moving like an old man, or a young man with stitches, Billy took the sterling silver star from Miss Kate and placed it on the top of their tree. "There you go." He stepped back to appraise their work. His grandmother had shanghaied him into helping her decorate the thing. They'd draped colorful strands of popcorn and dried cranberries around it then hung some dainty little hand sewn ornaments on the branches. "It's a beautiful tree, Miss Kate."

Decorating for Christmas should have lifted his mood, but his spirits were still in the cellar. Charlene was gone and it felt like she had taken a part of him with her. Apparently Miss Kate was feeling the absence, too. She wasn't as sprightly or talkative as usual. In fact, too many of their evenings lately had drifted into a silence of depressed, lonely thoughts. At least for him. Strange how a woman who had been here such a short time, a woman he hadn't even kissed, had left such an indelible mark on his heart.

He sighed and walked over to the fire. So much for the Christmas spirit. All the hands were coming in a few hours for Christmas Eve dinner and he felt like sitting alone in a dark room. He'd done all this—bought a ranch, set to raising cattle, started the foundations for a legacy—because he wanted to share it someday with his family. His flame of ambition hadn't exactly gone out, but it was dying, as if starving for oxygen.

Frustrated at being such a lovesick buffoon, he grabbed a poker and jabbed at the fire. *God, forgive me for wallowing in self-pity ... and loneliness.*

It is not good for man to be alone.

Doesn't appear to be much I can do about it, Father, unless You've got someone waiting in the wings.

He didn't even like thinking about that. Charlene had set something right in his heart. He couldn't imagine anyone else ever doing that. Funny, he'd never pictured himself as the Heathcliff type. He'd been willing to marry and have a family, but after what a certain red head in Defiance had done to him, he'd abandoned the hope of actually falling in love again. Charlene had healed him, heart and soul, and made herself a permanent part of him.

But life would go on, he told himself. In a while, she would be a faded, bittersweet thought.

Strange, how she felt so close tonight, though. Billy would have sworn he could even smell her. Her scent, something sweet and made of memories, like baby powder and vanilla, mixed with the earthy scent of pine in the room. He would give anything if he could turn around and see her—

That's when he heard the screams.

Charlene hugged herself, but she wasn't really cold. The fire warmed her body. She shivered over an emptiness in her heart. She could hear Billy's smooth, deep voice, the rustle of Miss Kate's skirt, the distant, muffled mooing of cattle. The sounds of home.

Home.

How could she have lived almost thirty years someplace else and not feel as comfortable there as she did on a ranch a hundred years in the past?

The soft crunch of snow reached her as someone approached the house. Charlene's heart trip-hammered in her chest. *What's the plan again?* A surge of adrenaline streaked through her veins. *Pray for the cavalry?* Now that she was here, alone, in the midst of reality, that seemed ... stupid.

He could kill me.

She swallowed and felt for the gun in her pocket. Insurance, in case things went wrong. Holding her breath, she rose to her feet and turned around.

She wasn't prepared to see him like this. Dale stood in the door way looming and grinning at her. The fire light danced eerily in the hollows of his eyes and cheeks, accentuated the shadow of the sneer on his lips. He looked *demonic.*

And she knew. *He is here to kill me.*

"What are you doing here, Charlene?" He stood like a guard at a prison entrance, legs spread apart, hands behind his back. His gaze roamed the room. "I mean, don't get me wrong. If I was going to pick a place to end our marriage, this would be it. But why are *you* here?"

She resisted the urge to lick her lips, a nervous habit he would feed on. "It's home to me for some reason."

"Ah," he nodded and slowly took a step toward her. "That's right. You said you wanted to go home for the holidays. But really," he scratched his eyebrow, "I sort of thought you meant Telluride."

Raw panic exploded in her head. *Oh, God, what have I done? Please protect me. Please help me get back to Billy.* Instinctively, the will to live, the fear of death, pushed away every other thought. She whipped the .38 out of her pocket and pointed it at Dale. "I don't know what I was thinking, but neither one of us should have come here."

He registered the gun in her hand and looked startled, but only for an instant. Then he pulled his lips into a thin, tight line and sighed, an exasperated sound as if he really didn't have time for this. "Charlene, you know, I did kind of love you … for a while. But you're just too headstrong. You wouldn't obey." He took another step. "You swore you'd obey me. You swore to that God you love so much and you swore to me."

"Marriage is a partnership, Dale, not indentured servitude."

His teeth clenched. "You swore you'd obey me." He put his hand out to her. "If you would have just obeyed, I wouldn't have had to beat you."

Charlene instinctively took a step back and Dale morphed into a blur of motion. He lunged and swiped at her, knocking the gun out of her hand then his fingers gouged down into her shoulder. The back of his other hand slammed into the side of her face, snapping her head to the right. She didn't freeze like usual. This time, fury turned her blood to lava. She screamed with rage and lashed out with a vengeance, kicking him in the groin and ramming her elbow into his nose as he bent over. Bellowing in pain, he doubled over but clutched and grasped for her as she tried to get past him. Clawing frantically for any piece of her, he tangled his fingers in her hair and yanked.

Charlene nearly fell backward into him, but she managed to twirl instead and duck his oncoming fist. Almost hysterical to get away from him, she squirmed and flailed like a wildebeest caught in the jaws of a crocodile. Screaming and growling, she let the memory of every beating fuel her fight.

She kicked and clawed and punched. She laced her fingers together and pounded her hands into the side of his head like a sledge hammer.

She simply didn't have the strength, though, to overpower him. Dale shook off her attack and jabbed Charlene in the mouth with a big, heavy fist. Stars of pain sputtered and burst in her mouth followed by the taste of blood. She roared like an animal and tried to claw at his face, but Dale grabbed her throat and shoved her hard into the hearth. The back of her head slammed into the stone and teeth-jarring agony reverberated through her brain. Through her double vision, she saw Dale pull his hand back, aiming to deliver a vicious blow.

Suddenly, he was snatched back from behind. Startled, he thrashed about, howling furiously. Charlene shook her head and blinked in disbelief.

Billy?

Billy pulled his hand back high over his head and hit Dale so hard, her husband's head snapped back with a cracking sound. He staggered into the wall, shook his head, and clawed at the wallpaper for support. Billy stepped closer to Charlene, putting his back to her and facing Dale. "Are you all right?" he asked over his shoulder.

Joy tangled up in her throat. He was here! "Yes."

Sneering, Dale wiped a smear of blood across his lips and drew himself up to his full height, which still left him a few inches shorter than Billy. There was plenty of fire in his eyes, though, and it burned brightly, unmistakably. "Who are you?"

"The man who's gonna bury you if you ever touch her again."

Dale chuckled and heaved a deep breath. He swayed, but only slightly, as his gaze whipped back and forth between her and Billy. "So is he your lover, Charlene? You've been cheating on me?" He sounded incredulous.

Billy subtly wiggled his fingers behind his thigh, motioning for Charlene to come closer. She pressed up against him, clutching a pleat in his vest. He reached back and rested his hand on the small of her back, his touch flooding her with peace. "Any man that would hit a woman deserves to be eaten by wolves. If I had time, I'd tie you out for bait."

"You think you're going somewhere, tough guy?"

Billy only hesitated a moment. "If she's going with me ... I believe so." He turned his head but didn't take his attention off Dale. "It's your call, Charlene."

Joyous. No other word described how she felt. She clutched Billy's shoulder and nodded. He wanted her with him, but her husband needed to understand the situation. "Dale, there's a marshal in town who has a letter I wrote. If anything happens to my parents, or if he ties you to any crime at all in Telluride ... his badge won't stop him from finding you."

Dale sucked in his cheeks and studied her and Billy. "Well, I guess there's only one thing I can do then." Dale reached behind his back, tugged at his waistband and whipped out a menacing black Glock. The world shifted into slow motion. All at once, Billy spun and covered Charlene with his body. She screamed and saw the flash of fire from the barrel as the gun thundered.

God, please save—

CHAPTER 14

*D*ale fired as the man shielded Charlene …

The bullet ricocheted off the fireplace, blowing out a chunk of river rock. Dale quickly took a step back and waved the gun around the room … but he was alone. The room was empty.

How the …

"Drop your gun, Dale!"

Panicked, confused, Dale whirled and fired the .44 in the direction of the voice. A hailstorm of bullets accompanied by their own thunder rained down on him. The remaining pieces of glass in the bay window shattered. He twitched and flailed as the burning stabs of lead sunk deep in his chest and side and shoulder. The gun slipped from his hand and Dale dropped to his knees. The rain of bullets stopped.

In a deafening silence, he looked down at his chest and watched a red stain bloom.

Wasn't supposed to end this way …

Wheezing, his lungs laboring for air, his mind clouded. An overwhelming desire for sleep came over him and he lay down on the hundred-year-old-floor. A coppery taste filled his mouth. A man leaned over him, a man in a black baseball hat and thick coat. He reached down and touched Dale's neck. After a moment, he pressed the mic at his shoulder. "Walt, the shooter is down. Get the paramedics to meet us ..."

Dale reached up and grabbed the man's shoulder, shocked that his arm felt like it weighed a thousand pounds. "Charlene ...? Where is ...? Couldn't have missed. Point ... blank ... range. "

The man looked around and then leaned into Dale, his jaw tensed. "Apparently you missed, Dale ... But I didn't."

Dale frowned. He didn't understand, he wanted to ask ... but he was so sleepy ... and the cold was seeping into his bones. His arm lost its strength and flopped to the floor.

"I don't think you're gonna make it, Dale. We'll get you down off this mountain as fast as we can, but if I were you ... I'd make my peace with God." The man hit the mic again. "I need some help. I think we're moving a corpse, but let's get it done."

CHAPTER 15

*T*he thunder echoed …

Billy and Charlene tumbled to the floor. He landed on top of her and they froze, lost in each other's eyes. Glass shattered and they jerked their heads toward the sound, expecting to see Dale. Instead, Miss Kate stood next to the Christmas tree, the shards of an ornament littering the rug at her feet. Her right hand was poised in mid-air, as if she'd been holding the decoration. Her mouth was agape in a perfect little circle.

Charlene dropped her head to the ground and started laughing. She was alive and she was home! Billy laughed, too, though he sounded more relieved than amused. Holding her gaze, he climbed to his feet and brought her with him. "Will you stay this time? I mean," he ducked his chin humbly, "if you want to be here."

Charlene raised her hand to his cheek and forced her voice to work. "I came back hoping …" She swallowed against the lump in her throat. "Praying. Praying that God would bring me back. Praying that you even wanted me."

Billy clutched the hand at his cheek. "I don't understand any of this, Charlene. I don't need to. Just promise me you'll never leave again."

Unable to hold back the tears, she nodded. "I promise." From the corner of her eye, she saw Miss Kate wipe tears from her cheeks.

God, I don't know why You've done this for me, but thank You. I'll never forget it.

Billy grinned. His throat bobbed. "Dang," he whispered, sounding mystified. "I don't know what all I did to deserve this, but–" She cut him off with a kiss, grabbing his stubbly cheeks between her hands and standing up on her tiptoes to reach him. He kissed her back, firmly and possessively, then picked her up and spun her around. "I can't think of a better Christmas present."

Charlene hugged his neck and savored the feel of his muscles beneath her fingers. She breathed him in. He smelled like pine, and leather, and maybe a touch of lilac water. He smelled like Heaven.

"Well, I'd better check on those cookies," Miss Kate said smiling broadly, her chin quivering. She lifted her skirt and side-stepped the glass at her feet. "And get the broom." As she walked past the pair, Billy set Charlene down and Miss Kate paused. "I can't tell you how glad I am that you're back." She raised a brow and shot Billy a mischievous look. "One more day of his moping and I was going to the sanitarium." She huffed and continued on into the kitchen.

Billy grinned and rubbed Charlene's arms. "She's right. When you left, the way you left, it felt like … my whole life got derailed. I can't explain it but—"

She touched her fingers lightly to his lips. "Don't try. It's a gift." She drifted into his arms, certain she had found her future here in the past. "I think we're just supposed to say thank you."

"And Merry Christmas."

"And Merry Christmas," she echoed.

"And I love you."

Her breath hitched and Billy lowered his chin, waiting. Charlene smiled slowly. "And I love you."

EPILOGUE

$\mathcal{L}$inda and Nathan stared at the safe deposit box held in the gnarled, spotted hands of Milton Barwell, the oldest practicing attorney in Telluride.

"I wondered if I would ever get to deliver this box."

Barwell's voice was raspy and weak. Nathan wondered how the man had managed to live this long, much less work into his eighties. Should he even be driving?

"Again, please forgive me for interrupting your Thanksgiving Day festivities, but my client was adamant that I get this to you today."

Reaching across the coffee table, he handed the couple the metal container, the size of a shoe box. Linda took it hesitantly, questioning Nathan with her eyes. He nodded and she set it in her lap.

"It's been in my safe since February of 1965. I am pleased and gratified that I've been able to see her instructions to completion. Charlene Page was quite a fixture in this town." Nathan heard his wife gasp … or maybe that was him.

"I was wondering," the old attorney's voice dropped to a conspiratorial tone, "if you would allow me to be present when you open it. You can't imagine my curiosity after all these years."

Nathan nodded, more out of shock than actual acquiescence. Cautiously, as if she half-expected a snake to jump out, Linda lifted the lid on the box. She hesitated only a moment before removing an envelope addressed to her and Nathan. He recognized the handwriting immediately.

The lawyer leaned in, overwhelmed by his curiosity. "Charlene wasn't a doctor, or so she always told folks, but she was the only medical person in Summit County until the fifties. She pushed for the ambulance service that finally got started in the sixties. Not to mention, her husband ran a fine ranch until his death in '57. The same year I came to Telluride."

Nathan had tuned him out. He watched breathless as Linda pulled an old newspaper clipping from the box. Beneath it, he saw several more newspaper clippings, the edges of photographs, and what looked like a journal. Linda carefully unfolded the clipping in her hand, mindful that it looked old and was rather brittle. Cut from the long-extinct Telluride Times, a typically somber couple in their wedding attire stared benignly into the camera.

Stunned, Nathan snatched his eye glasses from his pocket, slid them on, and leaned in for a closer look. He knew the bride. There was no mistaking Charlene, even in the lovely, bustled Victorian gown. The tight curls framing her face and upswept hairdo didn't change her look enough that he didn't know his own daughter. And the young man? Was he her husband? Confused, he glanced at the date at the top of the page. June 6, 1904.

"My," Barwell said, looking down his nose through his spectacles, "she bears a striking resemblance to your daughter, doesn't she?"

Nathan almost laughed at the old man's observation. He

didn't understand this. Couldn't explain it in anyway. But Nathan Williams, a simple, Godly man pastoring a small church of a hundred souls, knew one thing for sure. He squeezed Linda's hand, rejoicing that God had allowed his daughter to give them something so very special for Thanksgiving. "She found a way, Linda. Praise the Lord, she found a way."

*I*f you liked *In Time for Christmas*, I cannot tell you how much I would **appreciate your review!** Authors on Amazon literally live and die by those things! If you could take a moment, you will have my undying gratitude.

Please subscribe to my newsletter to receive updates on my new releases and other fun news. You'll also receive a FREE ebook—

A Lady in Defiance, The Lost Chapters

just for signing up! We have a lot of fun with my newsletter so I hope you'll join us.

And now, for a BONUS!
Here's the first chapter from my newest time travel Christmas story, ***For the Love of Liberty***! I hope you enjoy it.
You can get your complete copy here!

hiladelphia
1776

*R*edcoats filled the tavern, their chatter and clanking silverware making it difficult for Martin and Silas Hemsworth to talk. Martin leaned forward and repeated his comment, louder this time. "I said I am exceedingly proud of you, Silas. I'm sure England will win the war tomorrow, now that you've enlisted."

Silas's chin came up and Martin would have sworn he puffed out his chest another three inches. The British uniform fit to a T, adding years of maturity to a boy of eighteen. If only his little brother were as wise as he looked. Martin, however, would not share his doubts today.

"Thank you, brother." Silas, almost a mirror image of Martin with jet black hair, deep blue eyes, and a broad, tall frame, beamed at the compliment. "I'm glad I went with the regulars as opposed to the Dragoons. I think we'll see more action."

A chill of fear skittered up Martin's spine and he was glad they'd sat near the fireplace. The Hemsworth sons got their hair color from their Shawnee mother but their recklessness from their Irish father. Silas had yet to tame the beast. "You'll forgive me if I pray every day that you're bored senseless the length of your enlistment."

As they laughed at the comment, Prudence, the tavern owner, delivered their ales. "These are on the house. In honor of you joining the army, Silas."

A young widow with delicate features, dark, auburn hair, and bewitching brown eyes, she had done well to hang on to her tavern *and* her virtue. Martin suspected most women would have traded one or the other when the city fell, but she had fearlessly put an arrogant Lieutenant Lewis in his place. Promising him separation from important body parts if he touched her or her tavern, she'd brandished a knife to shore up the threat. Martin's timely interruption had forced the lieutenant to retreat, and now he suspected the soldier was nursing a grudge.

Still, Prudence's tenacity was worthy of admiration and he raised his ale to her, wishing again he felt like pursuing her. "Thank you, my dear friend," he said.

"Yes, thank you, thank you," Silas chimed in. Prudence squeezed his shoulders and left to tend to her customers. Both brothers watched her go, appreciative of her looks and temperament. "Brother, why have you not attempted to win Prudence's affections? She's a fine catch."

Martin dragged his focus back to his drink. "Prudence needs a man who can hold his tongue and his temper." He did not attempt to hide his self-loathing. "Until I am sure of myself, I'm not fit company."

"You mean until you've flagellated yourself enough." Silas smacked the table. "Good Lord, brother, be done with this. It's been over a year. Would you have preferred both Mother and Father had died at the hands of those ruffians? Of course not. You did what you had to do."

Martin wished he could make Silas understand. He feared war might. "Fighting is one thing, Silas. Blind fury is another. I nearly killed that man."

"But you didn't." He guzzled his beer and banged the empty mug down on the table. Wiping his mouth with the back of his hand, he smacked his lips loudly. "I'd take blind fury over paralyzing fear any day. Especially in a fight."

"It's unacceptable to lose your wits in either direction. Self-control is the mark of a strong, steady man."

Silas shook his head and sighed. "I don't know what else to say to you, brother."

A group of soldiers passed their table, revealing in their wake a servant girl standing nearby. Martin noticed her instantly. A pretty little thing, petite and curvy, but not so young. Closer to his age of thirty. A gold braid hung free of her mob cap. Wide, green eyes scanned the tavern with what he would have described as awe. Her delicate, pink mouth hung open, giving her an expression of an overwhelmed child on Christmas morn. When did Prudence hire her?

Silas tracked his brother's gaze and slapped his mug into the girl's stomach. "Wench, more ale."

Speechless, she took the mug and followed Silas's red-clad arm to meet his gaze. She gawked at him and he frowned at her. "Do you not speak the King's English, woman? More beer."

"Silas, don't be rude," Martin scolded. Perhaps all the soldiers made the poor girl nervous, he guessed. "Can't you see she's overwhelmed?" He offered her a warm smile. "I must apologize for my little brother here. He's only just arrived in Philadelphia. Hasn't even broken in the uniform yet. I fear he's a bit full of himself."

"Oh. My. God," the girl whispered. "I'm here and it's so real." She sounded stunned.

Vexed by her strange comment, Martin and Silas both stared, at a loss for words. Then the young lady did the strangest thing. She reached out and plucked at Silas's sleeve, as if she'd never seen a redcoat before. Seemingly oblivious to his befuddled expression, she turned her attention to Martin, studying his attire. A cooper and cabinetmaker, he was wearing his homespun shirt and leather work apron. Now he wished he'd worn his nicer waistcoat instead.

Her scrutiny climbed to his face and their eyes locked. Something in Martin fluttered to life, or at least sparked.

Long, coffee-colored lashes framed the brightest jade eyes he'd ever seen. And skin as smooth as silk, touched with a hint of peach, begged for a caress. He realized he was staring and collected his wits. "Madame, are you all right?"

"What's your name?"

The abruptness of the question at first startled him, but clearly she was reminding him of his manners. Chastised, he sought the proper formality. "Martin Hemsworth. And whom do we have the pleasure of addressing?"

A boisterous group of soldiers, heading out, chose that moment to cut between them and when they cleared, the girl was gone. Martin looked everywhere. He stood and scanned the tavern. How could she—?

"She must have gone into the kitchen." Scowling, Silas bent down and retrieved his mug from the floor. "I think she's slow-witted. Terrible choice for a tavern wench. And I still need more ale."

Puzzled, Martin slowly retook his seat. He caught Prudence by the arm as she passed. "Who is the new servant girl? I think she's struggling to handle your crowd."

Prudence pulled back, scrunching her face at him. "What new servant girl?"

"She was just here. Very pretty blonde."

"Who did not take my mug and refill it," Silas complained, holding it up for Prudence.

"I don't know what you're both going on about, but..." She plucked the cup from Silas's hand. "One more on the house."

She disappeared into the boisterous crowd and Martin flinched. "You oaf. You mistook a patron for a wench. She probably ran out of here in humiliation."

Silas scowled. "Uh, I believe you made the same assumption."

"Yes, I suppose I did." Martin looked the room over again,

hoping he would see her, knowing nothing could come of it, but hoping nonetheless.

*I*f you'd like to finish reading **For the Love of Liberty**, you can get your copy today! And thank you!

~Reluctant Romantics Anthology~

LOVE, LIES, & TYPEWRITERS—Book 1

A cowboy with a Purple Heart. A reporter with a broken heart. Which one is her Mr. Right?

When Lucy Daniels is rescued from a stampeding herd of cattle by war hero Dale Sumner, sparks fly and headlines are born. Smelling an opportunity, the local newspaper decides to send the couple on a tour selling war bonds—and subscriptions. Enamored with her handsome savior, Lucy is happy to play her part … until she realizes she may be falling in love with the wrong man.

Ace reporter and aspiring mystery writer Bryce Richard is tasked with building up Lucy and Dale's budding affair. He can't think of anything worse for a journalist than switching from hard news to pounding out romantic drivel. The task is especially hard when he wishes Lucy would look to him for her happily-ever-after.

When love and lies collide on the front page, will Lucy and Bryce have a chance to write their own fairytale ending? Or are they already yesterday's news? A heartwarming romance worthy of the Hallmark Channel, Love, Lies, & Typewriters is a funny, inspirational story of love and courage at a transformational time in America.

ROMANCE, REALITY, AND BLOG WRITERS—Book 2

A story about rediscovering faith and finding love in the place you least expect it ...

~Brides of Blessings Series~

COMING FEB. 14, 2018!

HELL-BENT ON BLESSINGS—Book 3

ALSO ...

Please be sure to check out the other books in the Gold Rush-era *Brides of Blessings* series. These are stories of women who weren't looking for marriage, but are instead forging through hardships to set down roots in California. The pioneer ladies here are independent, hard-working, and not so easy to romance. Likewise, the men in Blessings are from all walks of life. They have come west seeking redemption, fortunes and new beginnings. **Somehow, love always enters in ...**

~Lockets & Lace Series~

LOCKET FULL OF LOVE—Book 5

Was her husband a sinner or a saint? A traitor or a spy?

For years Juliet Watts has believed her husband died saving nothing more than a cheap trinket--but the locket he risked his life for turns out to hold a mysterious key. Together, Juliet and military intelligence officer Robert Hall go on a journey of riddles and revelations. But Juliet is convinced Robert is hiding something, too. Maybe it's just his heart ...

~Romance in the Rockies Series~

A LADY IN DEFIANCE—Book 1

His town. Her god. Let the battle begin.

Charles McIntyre owns everything and everyone in the lawless, godless mining town of Defiance. When three good, Christian sisters from his beloved South show up stranded, alone, and offering to open a "nice" hotel, he is intrigued enough to let them stay...especially since he sees feisty middle sister Naomi as a possible conquest. But Naomi, angry with God for widowing her, wants no part of Defiance or the saloon-owning, prostitute-keeping Mr. McIntyre. It would seem however, that God has gone to elaborate lengths to bring them together. The question is, "Why?" Does God really have a plan for each and every life?

Written with gritty, but not gratuitous, realism uncharacteristic of historical Christian fiction, A Lady in Defiance gives a nod to both Pride and Prejudice and Redeeming Love. Based on true events, it is also an ensemble piece that deftly weaves together the relationships of the three sisters and the rowdy residents of Defiance.

Book One of the best-selling Romance in the Rockies series, *A Lady in Defiance* is reminiscent of longstanding western fiction classics.

HEARTS IN DEFIANCE—Book 2

Men make mistakes. God will forgive them. Will their women?

Charles McIntyre built the lawless, godless mining town of Defiance practically with his bare hands ... and without any remorse for the lives he destroyed along the way. Then a glimpse of true love, both earthly and heavenly, changed him. The question is, how much? Naomi Miller is a beautiful, decent woman. She says she loves McIntyre, that God does, too, and the past is behind them now. But McIntyre struggles to believe he's worth saving ... worth loving. Unfortunately, the temptations in Defiance only reinforce his doubts.

Billy Page abandoned Hannah Frink when he discovered she was going to have his baby ... and now he can't live with himself. Or without her. Determined to prove his love, he leaves his family and fortune behind and journeys to Defiance. Will Hannah take Billy back or give him what he deserves for the betrayal?

Gritty and realistic, this is the story of real life and real faith in Defiance.

A PROMISE IN DEFIANCE—Book 3

Choices have consequences. Even for the redeemed.

Reformed Saloon-Owner and Pimp...

When Charles McIntyre founded the Wild West town of Defiance, he was more than happy to rule in hell rather than serve in heaven. But things have changed. Now, he has faith, a new wife...and a ten-year-old half-breed son. Infamous madam Delilah Goodnight wants to take it all away from him. How can he protect his kingdom and his loved ones from her schemes without falling back on his past? How does he fight evil if not *with* evil?

Redeemed Gunman...

Logan Tillane carries a Bible in his hand, wears a gun on his hip, and fights for lost souls any way he can. Newly arrived in Defiance, he has trouble, though, telling saints from sinners. The challenge only worsens when Delilah flings open the doors to the scandalous Crystal Chandelier Saloon and Brothel. She and the new preacher have opposite plans for the town. One wants to save it, one wants to lead it straight to hell.

Reaping...

For Tillane and McIntyre, finding redemption was a long, hard road. God's grace has washed away their sins, but the consequences remain and God will not be mocked. For whatsoever a man soweth, that shall he also reap...and the harvest is finally at hand.

~Brides of Evergreen Series~

HANG YOUR HEART ON CHRISTMAS— Book 1

He wants justice--some say revenge. She wants peace. A deep betrayal may deny them everything.

As punishment for a botched arrest, U.S. Marshal "Dent" Hernandez is temporarily remanded to the quiet little town of Evergreen, Wyoming. Not only does his hometown hold some bad memories, but he is champing at the bit to go after vicious killers, not waste his time scolding candy thieves. And he most certainly should not be escorting the very pretty, but jittery, schoolteacher around. What is she so afraid of? Turns out, a lot of folks are keeping secrets in Evergreen.

An old-fashioned Western, Hang Your Heart on Christmas reads like an episode of Gunsmoke or Bonanza. Packed with drama, a tantalizing mystery, and a heartwarming romance, you'll come back to read this lawman's story again and again--a story you'd expect to see on the the Hallmark Channel but one with a mystery worthy of Longmire.

BONUS MATERIAL-- Includes a special vintage Christmas recipe and the true story behind the fictional Dent Hernandez! A clean, cowboy western romance with action and adventure. A great read, to take on vacation with you, any time of the year!

ASK ME TO MARRY YOU— Book 2

Here comes the bride ... and he's not happy

Audra Drysdale grudgingly accepts that the mere presence of a husband will keep her men working on her ranch, and a greedy cattle baron under control. It seems a perfectly reasonable idea, then, to ask her uncle, who is the town attorney and a matchmaker of sorts, to find her a groom--a "proxy" who will take her orders and dish them out to the men. A marriage of convenience seems to be in order ...

Dillon Pine is in jail for a conspiracy charge, but because of certain mitigating factors, he's deemed a good risk for an unusual form of probation: serving as Audra's husband. After a year, he can abandon her and she won't tell. By then, she will have proven to the cowboys she's a competent rancher, and the cattleman next door will be looking elsewhere for a wife. But when word gets out that Dillon came to Audra via Evergreen's matchmaker, he's dubbed a "male order bride." The resulting jokes at his expense are constant and brutal. Just how much abuse can Dillon's pride stand?

When Audra discovers her father's death was no accident, she realizes her new husband is in danger, too. And she cares . . . quite a lot, it turns out. To save Dillon, she may have to let go of the one thing she's fought her whole life to keep.

A heartwarming light comedy, Ask Me to Marry You tells a story in the vein of **Love Comes Softly** and **Pride and Prejudice**. Hope, courage, and selfless sacrifices - what you'll do for the man you love. Enjoy this sweet, "clean and wholesome" mail order bride story-- with a twist!

MAIL-ORDER DECEPTION—Book 3

Secret identities lead to stolen hearts.

Can love survive the truth?

Intrepid reporter Ellie Blair wants a story--the one story--that will make her name bigger than Nellie Bly's. She'll do anything to get it. Lie, masquerade as someone else ... even walk away from a man she could love.

A PROPOSAL SO MAGICAL—Book 4

Sometimes, it takes a truly strong man to surrender to love...

Evergreen's sheriff, Dent Hernandez, has to learn to live with love. Not an easy thing for a man who for years made a career of hunting down and hanging some of the worst outlaws in the territory. Can he find his romantic side and ask for Amy's hand in a truly unique, magical way?

Or will a suave, handsome ghost from her past derail Dent's plan—if he can even come up with one?

TO LOVE AND TO HONOR—Book 5

Faith. Honor. Love. Which will he sacrifice?

Joel Chapman feels like a failure. Losing a leg in battle, he failed to fulfill his duty as a captain. According to his wife, without two good legs, he's failed as a husband and provider. Along with his self-respect, his spirit is dying a slow, painful death.

Angela Fairbanks is the daughter of a tyrant—a cattle baron known for his iron fist and cold heart. She has no doubt once he learns she is carrying an illegitimate child, he will banish her from the ranch.

Compassion and honor overtaking his good sense, Joel offers a noble lie to protect Angela and secure a home for her and the baby: one day as her husband, and then he'll "abandon" her.

Will the noble lie become simple deceit? Or is he man enough to resist his heart and keep his vows?

IN TIME FOR CHRISTMAS – A NOVELLA

Charlene needs a miracle. God has one waiting ... a hundred years in the past.

Charlene needs a miracle to escape her abusive husband. Will traveling one hundred years in the past be far enough to get away?

In Time for Christmas is a haunting tale of love and hope set against the backdrop of turn-of-the-century Colorado. Reminiscent of Somewhere in Time and The Two Worlds of Jenny Logan, this quick page turner will reveal how each life has a purpose and plan.

Charlene Williams is a wounded woman trapped in a dangerously violent marriage. When husband Dale discovers her innocent chats with the mailman, he flies into a jealous rage and whisks her out of town to his family's ranch--an isolated, dilapidated place no one has lived on for years. With the promise that he'll be back in a few days, he knocks Charlene unconscious and leaves.

She wakes up on the ranch--a hundred years in the past. Almost instantly she is drawn to Billy Page, Dale's great grandfather. The connection is powerful and mysterious, but should she risk falling in love ... with a ghost?

She'll learn one thing for certain: Her Heavenly Father is in control of the very fabric of time.

GRACE BE A LADY

Act like a man. Think like a lady.

Banished to the dusty cow town of Misery for an alleged affair, Grace Hendrick wants nothing more than to get her son away from the clutches of his abusive father Bull, back in Chicago. But if she dares to return home, Bull has promised Grace she'll never see their son again. She has no choice but to accept her situation-- temporarily. Struggling to figure a way to survive, she refuses to consider prostitution. The hamlet of Misery, however, isn't brimming over with jobs for respectable women. Fueled by hate and desperation, she concocts a shocking plan to find work.

Thad Walker is the middle son of the oldest, most successful cattle baron in Wyoming, and he always puts the ranch first. One chance meeting with Grace Hendrick, though, batters his focus like a hail storm in July. And there couldn't be a worse time to lose his focus.

A true Western saga written in the the vein of Lonesome Dove and Redeeming Love, truth weaves seamlessly with fiction in Grace be a Lady to deliver a stunning tale of love blossoming in a field of violence.

~Sweethearts of Jubilee Springs Series~

A GOOD MAN COMES AROUND—Book 8

She has a list of qualifications for her groom.

He doesn't measure up.

But sometimes, a good man comes around.

Based on a true story ... Oliver Martin is a shiftless, mischievous no-account. But he wasn't always. Jilted at the altar, he takes nothing seriously anymore and now spends his days looking for a drink or trouble, whichever comes first. John Fowler, Oliver's friend and business partner, spends his time trying to keep Oliver out of trouble. Tired of rescuing the young man, Fowler decides a wife might bring back the old, steady Oliver. He applies for a mail order bride for the lad—but secretly.

Abigail Holt spent ten years married to a belligerent drunk. Now widowed, she's worn out trying to make ends meet and raise her boys alone. She has decided to become a mail order bride—in her estimation, the perfect way to pick a husband—using pure logic and a rational mind. Marrying for love the first time resulted in a train wreck. She wants to find a good man who is qualified to raise her sons. Romantic entanglements will not be part of the bargain.

She arrives in Jubilee Springs ready to wed Oliver—who has never heard of her. Perhaps that's a Godsend as he clearly doesn't meet her standards. The mail order fiasco ends Abigail's desire to ever be a bride again, and that's just fine with Oliver. He has no intention of ever getting his heart broken again.

But love and life—and even tragedy—can't be avoided. In fact, trying to run from them may do more harm than good …

ABOUT THE AUTHOR

"Heather Blanton is blessed with a natural storytelling ability, an 'old soul' wisdom, and wide expansive heart. Her characters are vividly drawn, and in the western settings where life can be hard, over quickly, and seemingly without meaning, she reveals Larger Hands holding everyone and everything together."

MARK RICHARD, *EXECUTIVE PRODUCER, AMC'S HELL ON WHEELS, and PEN/ERNEST HEMINGWAY AWARD WINNER*

A former journalist, Heather is an avid researcher and skillfully weaves truth in among fictional story lines. She loves exploring the American West, especially ghost towns and museums. She has walked parts of the Oregon Trail, ridden horses through the Rockies, climbed to the top of Independence Rock, and even held an outlaw's note in her hand.

She writes Westerns because she grew up on a steady diet of Bonanza, Gunsmoke, and John Wayne movies. Her most fond childhood memory is of sitting next to her father, munching on popcorn, and watching Lucas McCain unload that Winchester!

She can be reached several different ways:

http://ladiesindefiance.com/

https://www.facebook.com/
authorheatherblanton/?ref=hl
https://twitter.com/heatherfblanton
https://www.pinterest.com/heatherfblanton/

Christian Westerns is the genre that lets her write about strong pioneer women and men who struggle to find God and then live out their faith in real ways. Romance is always a strong element in her stories because it is such a beautiful gift from God, and a perfect reflection of how He loves His children: sacrificially and lavishly.

"I believe Christian fiction should be messy and gritty, because the human condition is ... and God loves us anyway."
-- Heather Blanton

Made in the USA
Las Vegas, NV
09 December 2023